Melinda
Takes a Hand

Melinda Takes a Hand

PATRICIA BEATTY

William Morrow and Company
New York 1983

Library of Congress Cataloging in Publication Data
Beatty, Patricia.   Melinda takes a hand.
Summary: In the year 1893, sensible thirteen-year-old Melinda, finding herself stranded in
the Colorado town of Goldendale, promptly becomes involved in the townspeople's lives and
assorted problems.
[1. West (U.S.)—Fiction. 2. Colorado—Fiction]
I. Title. PZ7.B380544Mf 1983 [Fic] 83-7971
ISBN 0-688-02422-X

To
the memory of
Samuel Reznick, M.D.,
gentleman and scholar
and
esteemed friend.

❦Contents❧

❧ I ❧
Edgar Everett Potter III
Enters Our Lives!

"This is for you, Melinda," said Aunt Rhoda, dangling a good-sized piece of yellow paper in front of my amazed eyes. It read:

> MELINDA ALBERTINE CARPENTER
> c/o CARPENTER'S FOUNDRY WORKS
> HURON STREET
> CHICAGO, ILLINOIS

At the top of the heavy paper was a hole at either edge, and between them was a piece of twine to make a loop. This was a sign to go around my neck. How horrible!

While my older sister, Sarah Jane, who was already twenty-six years old, looked on saying nothing to save me, Aunt Rhoda stepped forward to put the card over my head. She said, "Now hold still, child! Let's see how this looks and how it fits around your neck. I made it now so you can take it with you to Goldendale and then on to San Francisco. Just in case the stores out in California don't have such nice strong yellow paper yet."

As I backed away from her, she followed me, saying, "If you wear this on the train coming back from Sarah Jane's wedding in San Francisco, the conductors will look out for you all the way back home to Chicago. They'll put you in a hansom cab and have you sent to the foundry works where Uncle Julius will be waiting for you. With you wearing this, I won't have to worry about you traveling back to us all alone. Melinda, do stand still!" She and Uncle Julius, who was Papa's only brother, had taken Sarah Jane and me in and raised us when our parents died of yellow fever years ago. Aunt Rhoda always felt overly responsible for us.

But stand still and have her put a tag on me like I was going through the United States mail? I said through my gritting teeth, "I'm not a piece of parcel post! I promised to go with Sarah Jane, but not to wear any signs on me. If I go all the way out to California to see her marry Edgar Everett Potter, I ought to be able to get back to Chicago the same way all by myself without that tag on me." I took a deep breath and said what I often did to her, "After all, I'm thirteen years old now. I inherited the

Carpenter horse sense." My uncle hadn't said anything yet and I turned to him, asking, "Isn't that what people say, Uncle Julius—that I've got horse sense? It's 1893 now. I read the *Chicago Tribune,* too, you know. Trains aren't being attacked by Indians or the James brothers outlaws anymore."

As I'd figured, Uncle Julius was on my side. He scratched behind his left ear and said in his calm way, "Oh, Rhoda, Melinda's got a good head on her shoulders. She'll get back here just fine, I bet. She don't need to go parcel post. Anyhow, I think she's over the weight limit to go that way now."

Aunt Rhoda didn't think he was funny and pursed up her lips as she put the tag down on the parlor table. While I silently blessed Uncle Julius, I looked angrily out of the corner of one eye at my sister. Sarah Jane hadn't said one word in my favor about the tag. She should have! I might resemble the "family beauty," Sarah Jane, with yellow hair and gray eyes, but in character I wasn't like her. I had sense! I would never have got myself engaged to that old Edgar Everett Potter so fast it still made my head swim to think what she'd done. In fact, I wouldn't even have had Edgar roasted and set on a silver platter with a spiced crabapple in his jaws.

Even though she knew I was glaring at her at that very moment, she picked up the terrible tag and said, "Aunt

Rhoda, I think I'll take this along with me all the same. If Edgar thinks Melinda will need it, we'll have it ready for her when she starts home for Chicago alone."

Aunt Rhoda said, "Yes, that would save you from having to make another one. There's nothing like foresight!"

Foresight? I wanted to laugh out loud but didn't. My sister was planning to marry a man she'd known only for two weeks. Foresight, my left hind foot! Whatever common sense she had ever had left her the minute she set eyes on Edgar Everett Potter. She had fallen in love with him at first sight.

I knew! I'd been with her the day she met him. He was standing with his hands in his pockets in front of the California exhibition at the World's Columbia Exposition, which was held here in Chicago to celebrate Columbus's discovery of America four hundred years before. Sarah Jane and I had planned to go to the fair that afternoon, but we hadn't intended to visit the California exhibit until Aunt Rhoda, who had a sore bunion and couldn't come, told us to take a look at the unusual sculpture from California that the *Chicago Tribune* had written about. It was a knight on horseback, all made out of prunes. She thought it was something we two ought to see.

Well, I saw it and was disappointed, even if I hadn't

expected very much anyway. It was a big statue up on a wooden platform. The figures of the knight and his horse were covered with gold paint so you could only see the prunes as lumps under the paint. I couldn't see why they had painted the prunes and was about to say so to Sarah Jane when I noticed that she wasn't looking at the statue at all. She was more interested in the young man in the brown-striped summer suit and brown derby hat standing in front of it. Sarah Jane was twirling her parasol, laughing and tilting her head to one side. Flirting again! She'd been a flirt for years and years. I just hated to be around her when she was up to that.

I went over to her, tapped her on the arm, and said, "Sarah Jane, there's a show of big cannons I want to see in a building down the road. Uncle Julius said for me to see them!"

"Sarah Jane, eh?" said the man, who had a red-brown mustache, red-brown eyes, and a lean, freckly face. He asked me, "Well, how do you like the prune horse from California, little girl? It attracts a lot of attention, let me tell you."

I told him honestly, "I think it would be more interesting if it wasn't painted over. Nobody ever saw a gold horse."

He grinned at Sarah Jane and spoke to her. "Nobody ever saw a purple horse, either. I decided the statue had better be golden because California is called the golden state."

In her honey voice Sarah Jane asked him, "Did you do the sculpture?"

"Some of it, yes, ma'am, I did. Edgar Everett Potter had a hand in its creation. It's a tribute to California's agricultural industry. It's got 6256 large prunes to the horse and 2733 smaller ones to the rider."

My sister breathed, "How wonderful!" Then she told me, "Melinda Carpenter, you go see those cannons by yourself. I don't want to see them. Then come back here when you're done." She turned to the man once more and said, "My sister has little appreciation of artistic ability."

"Carpenter, eh?" He grinned, then said, "You must be Sarah Jane Carpenter, then. Do you live here in Chicago?"

"Oh, yes, all my life. . . ."

I didn't wait to hear anymore and went off to see the Krupp cannons. Uncle Julius, who owned a foundry, had been impressed by them, but I wasn't. I thought they were big and ugly, uglier even than the prune horse and rider. I hung around them for a time, though, so Sarah Jane could flirt in peace and get it out of her system.

That August afternoon was hot. By the time she and I finally got back onto the streetcar and headed for home, my feet hurt from my tight high-button shoes, and my arms ached from carrying the box of prunes Edgar Everett Potter had given Sarah Jane to take home. Once we were aboard the streetcar, my ears started to ache from all the talking my sister did about him. His name was Edgar Everett Potter III. He was twenty-nine years old. He'd been born in Colorado Territory, but lived in California now and worked in San Francisco doing something about "agriculture" out there. He was a Democrat, like Uncle Julius. His parents lived in Goldendale, Colorado, he was an only child, and, oh joy, he wasn't married or engaged to any lady.

"All right," I asked as I clutched at the box of prunes, which was slipping over my lap, "when's this Mr. Potter coming to call on you, Sarah Jane?"

"Tonight. We're going to hear John Philip Sousa's band at the exposition."

"But you're supposed to go to an ice cream social with somebody else, aren't you?" I could never keep up with my sister's beaux, so I didn't try to remember their names.

"Humbug to him, Melinda! I'll call him on the telephone and say I have a headache from the hot weather. The telephone is very useful."

I knew that. I used it a lot too, but not to tell fibs over. I said, "That's wrong of you, Sarah Jane."

This made her sit up very straight, frowning. "Yes, it *is* wrong, but Mr. Potter won't be here in Chicago much longer. He has to get back to his job now that the sculpture is made. He'll be going back to San Francisco soon, and wants to show me the whole fair and wants me to show him Chicago before he leaves. He's not like the other men I know, Melinda. He's special."

This made me say, "He's leaving his prune statue here? I thought he'd take it back to California with him." Then I laughed.

"Don't be ridiculous, and don't you make fun of Mr. Potter either. If you can't be polite when he comes to our house, Melinda, don't be present at all."

Oh, but Edgar Everett Potter could court a lady! None of Sarah Jane's Chicago beaux were half so speedy or half so extravagant. Maybe it was the California way to do it fast and spend plenty of money. Mr. Potter didn't ever use streetcars. Instead, he rented buggies whenever he called for Sarah Jane to take her dancing, to the fair, or to the theaters. He sent flowers to her every day, and on two Sundays he even sent some to Aunt Rhoda, who had had her doubts about him at first but soon got won over. He brought big boxes of chocolate bonbons for the family and cigars for Uncle Julius, and talked to him a lot about the very fine future he would have out in California where the "sun shone all the time."

On his last night in Chicago he brought a large, square amethyst ring, which Sarah Jane wore on her left hand. We all understood what it meant—she had promised to marry him. He had to get back to California, so there wouldn't be time to have Aunt Rhoda arrange a wedding here. Instead, they'd get hitched in California later.

She wasn't to go back to San Francisco with him when he went because he needed some time to find a bigger place for them to live; his old place was only one room. She would come out after he telegraphed her that everything was ready. On her way to California she was going to stop off in Goldendale, Colorado, to meet his folks. Uncle Julius and Aunt Rhoda were happy that he had suggested this, because they thought the Potters might go on with Sarah Jane to San Francisco after they got to know her. That way she would not be going alone. My aunt and uncle wanted to go to California, too, but they couldn't. Aunt Rhoda grieved over the fact that Uncle Julius couldn't leave Chicago because he was having trouble at the foundry with a crew of new workmen and with business falloff just now. And she couldn't leave him because she knew danged well that he was so flustered right now he would forget to take his daily dose of heart medicine if she didn't stand over him frowning with the pill bottle in one hand and a glass of water in the other. Besides, someone had to cook for Uncle Julius, and I didn't know how. So Sarah Jane was to set off alone—and she was certainly willing!

My, how the telegraph wires between California and Illinois buzzed. The boy delivering telegrams was at our house nearly every other day, and on the days in between

Sarah Jane was at the telegraph office wiring Edgar. Edgar never wrote her letters, but we guessed sending telegrams was the California way of doing things, the expensive way.

Finally Sarah Jane got the wire she was waiting for—to come west and become Mrs. Edgar Everett Potter III. She was out of her mind with happiness.

Not me, though. Not only would I miss my only sister, I was also worried about her going so far away to folks she didn't know.

Though she didn't let on to Sarah Jane, Aunt Rhoda was feeling the same way. The day before my sister was to leave, Aunt Rhoda called me into the kitchen after breakfast and shut the door. She said, "Melinda, I dreamed of my grandma again last night, the one who got scalped by an Indian in 1800. In my dream she pointed right to her scalped head, then at me. That's a bad omen. I think it's got something to do with Sarah Jane and the wedding. I think we Carpenters ought to take a hand in it some-how. I wish your uncle and I could go west, but we can't. Melinda, I want you to go out to California with your sister and see her get married. Then when you come back here after it's all over, you can tell us about everything. You've got some sense for a girl your age. You could represent the Carpenters. Can you lose two weeks of school?"

Could I? You bet, I could! I'd never been anywhere in

my life before and now Colorado, and then California, were being offered to me. I blessed Aunt Rhoda's dream. Sometimes when she saw her scalped grandma, bad things did happen. Would I take a hand? You bet. After all Aunt Rhoda and Uncle Julius did for us, I owed it to them to help if they wanted me to.

I said, "Sure, I could miss some school. I get an A in everything but choral singing, and my music teacher will be glad to have a rest from me. You can write my principal that we've got a family emergency and I can't come to school for a while."

"Melinda, I was sure I could count on you. As soon as I write the note to your principal, I'll start packing for you. You won't need new clothes like Sarah Jane. You can wear the pale green muslin dress you got for Easter to the wedding. If you stick a calla lily in the sash, it will look just fine."

The green dress was all right with me. To get to travel to the West I would have gone to the wedding in Uncle Julius's red-striped nightshirt. But then, before we were ready to leave for the train depot, Aunt Rhoda brought out the yellow tag to go around my neck. I had to sit on the bed and watch my sister and aunt pack it in one of Sarah Jane's six suitcases.

Though I'd looked forward to traveling, I couldn't say that I truly enjoyed our trip to Colorado. First of all, once we got on the train I had to keep an eye peeled for anyone who might try to flirt with my sister. I was always reading in the newspapers about mashers, men who flirted with strange ladies, getting arrested, and I decided it was up to me to preserve Sarah Jane from them. Of course, she shouldn't take up with a flirting man now that she was engaged to Edgar Everett Potter III, but I couldn't be absolutely sure she wouldn't. She'd been a flirter for a long time now, and that habit might be hard to break. And, after all, she had let Mr. Potter mash her. I hadn't been on guard at the fair, but I would be on the train. If I saw anybody start to play up to her, I planned to tell the conductor immediately and have the man thrown off the train, even if we were right in the middle of nowhere.

My watchfulness worked up to a point. I saw men going through our car who looked like would-be flirts. They gawked at Sarah Jane, tipped their hats and smiled until they saw me beside her staring at them with what Aunt Rhoda called my "fish-eye" look. It was a sort of cold glare I had practiced in the mirror. After I gave them that, the men moved along and sat down somewhere else.

To give Sarah Jane credit, she didn't play up to any of those men. But to my horror, she did seem to take a shine to the blue-coated conductor himself, the man I planned to use as an ally, even though I couldn't say she was exactly flirting. He started to hang around our seats laughing and talking to Sarah Jane, who laughed along with him. He was a handsome black-haired man, but he seemed to me to be dull minded. Though I glared at him every time he came near us, it didn't do any good. I was upset. How could I complain to the conductor about himself being a masher and ask him to leave his own train?

So I did something else. I waylaid him out of Sarah Jane's sight at one end of our car and told him, "I think I'd better tell you that my sister is engaged to be married, in case you thought that purple ring on her hand wasn't really a ring of betrothal."

He grinned and said, "I figured that out myself a long time back. Now, little lady, is there anything wrong with my talking to a pretty lady on my train? I always talk to the pretty ladies. My wife knows about it. She doesn't mind."

Well, I doubted this was true, but I only said, "All right, then. But if somebody tries to mash Sarah Jane, will you get him off the train?"

"If she complains to me about somebody, I will have a little talk with him." He was still grinning as he asked me, "What about somebody flirting with you, honey?"

"I don't flirt. I will never flirt. If somebody is crazy enough to try to flirt with me, I want you to toss him off the train, too. And don't call me honey."

He laughed again, and I walked back to our seat and sat down, satisfied except for having been called honey. I didn't tell Sarah Jane what I'd done.

The train lurched and bumped along and sometimes its motion almost made me feel sick to my stomach. The ride was monotonous, and I didn't find the landscape interesting. We traveled through hundreds of miles of brown and yellow prairie without seeing any of the buffalo herds that should have been somewhere in view. Instead, we saw fields and fences and farmhouses, and one town after another. Neither were there any Indians galloping past on their ponies. Those we saw were sitting motionless, wrapped up in blankets, on station platforms. I was disappointed; I had expected a lot from the West I had read about in James Fenimore Cooper's books.

The train was dirty, and when we opened the window next to us dust blew in. The food in the dining car wasn't like Aunt Rhoda's cooking, and in my estimation, it cost too much money.

But neither the dull scenery, mashers and conductor, the food, or the dirt was as bad as the danged Horton Reclining Chairs we sat in for two and a half days. Sarah Jane had chosen them over Pullman berths in order to save money to set up housekeeping in California. Mr. Horton's chairs were supposed to be as "comfortable as rocking chairs in a person's own parlor," but after sitting in one all night, I decided Mr. Horton was either a liar or he had never sat in his own chairs. Though they tilted a bit, they didn't rock at all, and after twenty-four hours in one, I ached all over. When the train stopped, Sarah Jane and

I got off and stretched our legs on the station platform. We walked together, complaining how we felt. Because she was twice my age and getting on a bit in life, she groaned more than I did.

She told me, "I'm going to get berths for us when we take the train from Goldendale to San Francisco. I never want to hear the name of Horton again."

I agreed. "Let's give Mr. Pullman's invention a chance next time. Good health comes before thrift, I guess. I'm walking like I'm ninety-three, not just thirteen."

❧ 2 ❧
The Chicken Tracker

I wondered if we'd recognize Edgar Everett's folks when we reached the Goldendale train station. They were supposed to be waiting for us because Aunt Rhoda was going to telegraph them about our arrival once we left Chicago.

I recognized them right off. Mrs. Potter really didn't have to open and close her lavender parasol three times to attract our attention. Both of the Potters looked like Edgar Everett. Mrs. Potter had given him his red-brown hair, and his pa had given him the mustache that went up on one side and down a bit on the other. She wore a long, oyster-colored linen duster to keep dust off her duds, and he wore a tan one.

"Sally!" cried Mrs. Potter, as she came surging forward to embrace Sarah Jane, who had never been called Sally

16

in her whole life. Mr. Potter watched his wife, grinning. Then Mrs. Potter spotted me standing alone and asked, "Sally, who is the girl here? We had expected just you."

As I stood among the seven suitcases the porter had just set down, I said, "Me, I'm Melinda. I'm her sister."

Mrs. Potter turned to Mr. Potter II and said, "Well, we could put them in the guest bedroom together."

I told her, "That would be just fine. Our aunt Rhoda in Chicago sent me along to represent the Carpenter family at my sister's wedding."

Mr. Potter, who had sharp, dark eyes, said with a chuckle, "So, you're the family watchdog, eh?"

"You might say that. I take a hand in family doings." That ought to hold him. Then, as I looked around the platform and spied the telegraph office, I added, "I'd better telegraph our folks in Chicago that we got here. They'd like to know that. How much does a telegram cost in Goldendale? To send ten words costs thirty cents in Chicago."

"The price is the same all over the country," said Mr. Potter. "Have you got the cash with you?"

I lifted my pocketbook and jingled it. "I always keep some cash on hand. Mr. Potter, do you think they'd let me send a telegram for less? My message will be shorter than ten words."

"I doubt it," he told me, grinning.

I sighed. Western Union was not fair. All I planned to
say was, "We got here," which should have cost only nine
cents.

I started down the platform in the hot sunshine, but
stopped as two very tall young men with yellow hair and
small yellow mustaches, who looked enough alike to be
brothers, came up the steps at the end of the platform and
strode toward me and the Potters. They were dressed in
brown-and-yellow checkered jackets, tan riding breeches,
brown boots, and funny-looking brown hats that went
down in front and back.

One of them sang out in a loud, high-pitched,
strangely accented voice, "Oh, Potter! Eh, Potter! What
about our west tower?"

The other one, who sounded a lot like the first one,
called, "Weren't the stones for our castle's tower on this
train?" He came up to Mr. Potter and stood over him,
teetering on his toes and heels like he was nervous. "Mr.
Potter, we've been waiting a whole month for the stones
for the west tower. The east tower, the two wings, and
the central portion have already been set up. Egad, man.
You are our agent. You know we need that west tower!"

I stood staring at Mr. Potter. He'd put his hands deep
into the pockets of his duster and was teetering also. "No,
your stones were not on this train, Mr. Alfred and Mr.
Albert. I just now checked with the freight agent about
them. They'll probably be on the next train from the East

due the day after tomorrow. If they aren't here by then, I'll telegraph New York City and see what's happened. I'm sure the crates aren't still on the docks there. The rest of your castle came through just fine from England, so the tower will, too. How are things out at the ranch, Mr. Alfred?"

"Tolerable, tolerable, except for the west tower. The American workers you hired for us and our own Scottish menservants are getting us settled bit by bit," replied the one named Alfred. As he'd spoken, he took a piece of round glass out of his jacket pocket, squeezed it into his right eye, and held it there by squinting. He squinted fiercely at me for an instant, then for a long time at Sarah Jane, who was talking with Mrs. Potter. Finally, he asked Mr. Potter, "I say, who is that handsome gel, Potter?"

"My son's bride-to-be."

"A pity, that. Wouldn't you agree, Bertie?"

"A pity, indeed," came from Mr. Albert. "The gel's a little beauty." Mr. Albert hadn't stuck any glass into his eye to see Sarah Jane, so I reckoned he had better eyesight than his brother.

I held my breath. Were they about to try to mash on Sarah Jane in front of the Potters and me, too?

No, they turned on their heels together and walked past me down the platform steps out of sight. I came back to Mr. Potter to ask, "Who were they? Did they really expect a tower to come in on this train?"

He nodded. "They sure did. They're the Farnsworth-Jones brothers, remittance men from England. I sold them a ranch five miles out of town last year, and now they're erecting a castle on it. Their old papa back in England is shipping them one he doesn't need. It's being taken down there stone by stone and shipped in crates across the Atlantic Ocean and out here to Colorado. Each stone is marked where it ought to go."

"Why don't they build a new stone house?"

"They say a new house wouldn't be the same as the home they'd had as boys in England."

I pondered this, then said, "No, I guess not. Isn't a whole castle awful big, though?"

"I'd say it was, but aren't most castles large?"

"I guess maybe they are. By the way, you just called them remittance men, Mr. Potter. What does that mean?"

"Men who have disgraced their families in England and been sent away. They receive money from home to stay away."

My, this was very interesting. I'd never heard of paying anybody to keep away. I asked, "What did they do that was disgraceful?"

He sighed. "They're both called honourables. That means they're the sons of some nobility in England, maybe a duke. Mr. Albert told me that he disgraced himself by dancing with one of Queen Victoria's granddaughters at a ball while he was inebriated. I don't know what Mr. Alfred did to make himself a remittance man, too."

"What does *inebriated* mean, Mr. Potter?"

"Drunk."

I nodded. I wondered if Mr. Albert had tried to mash on the princess while dancing with her. "Are you sure you don't know what Mr. Alfred did?"

"Nope."

"That's too bad. It could be very interesting to tell Aunt Rhoda and Uncle Julius about later on. Well, I better go send my telegram now."

After I'd sent the telegram and had to pay out the full thirty cents, we got into the Potters' four-seater wagon and drove through Goldendale behind their team of sorrels. The town didn't impress me much. After having lived all my life in elegant Chicago, I had some ideas about what a city ought to be like. Goldendale was flat like Chicago, but instead of having a lake to the south of it, it had a mountain sticking up out of nowhere to the west, and beyond it a whole row of mountains. To the north were even more in the far distance. On the east side of town was the prairie, miles and miles of it.

I knew from my history lessons that Colorado wasn't an old state, so I hadn't expected Goldendale to be big. It wasn't. We rode down the main street, and I spotted telephone poles, three banks, nine saloons, four general stores, hotels, some feed stores, two churches, a newspaper office, barbers, dressmakers, lawyers' and doctors' offices, a schoolhouse, and a fire station. That was about what I had expected the center of town to look like.

At the end of the street, we turned left down one lined with what Mrs. Potter called "beauteous cottonwood trees." I had noticed something while we went down the big street, and asked the Potters about it. "Did you ever notice that the two churches we just passed look the same, and that the fire station and the school look alike, too?"

Mr. Potter twisted around in the front seat to say, "You've got a good eye, Missy. They *are* the same. The new city hall we put up just last year is just like the churches. A lot of the buildings here are prefabricated. They were ordered from a catalog and arrived as precut lumber. Carpenters here in Goldendale put them together. They go up fast, and are cheap to boot. The remittance brothers' castle isn't the only thing that comes in pieces. Our house is just like four others at our end of this street."

I kept quiet, but I couldn't help thinking this wasn't how things got built in Chicago. Folks there started from scratch.

Mrs. Potter added, "We ordered model 42-A, with the bay window and the veranda. We painted ours buff, though. All the others are plain old white, because that was the only color paint Mr. Mittelman had when the houses were put up. We went all the way to Denver for our paint."

Well, I could see where Edgar Everett got his artistic nature—from his mother who had to have a special-colored house.

As we got down out of the wagon in front of the buff house, Sarah Jane asked me in a whisper, "Well, what do you think of the Potters?"

I whispered back, "I don't know yet. Wait and ask me after supper. I think better on a full stomach."

"Melinda, behave yourself! While you were sending that telegram, Mrs. Potter told me that there is a letter for me from Edgar. Just think, it is the very first letter I have ever had from him. Did you notice that he never once wrote me?"

Of course I had, and so had Aunt Rhoda and Uncle Julius. We had all wondered if he'd busted his arm the minute he got back to California, and so couldn't write.

Sarah Jane and I followed Mrs. Potter up the front walk between red rose bushes, while Mr. Potter took the wagon back to the small barn behind the house. It was the same style barn I'd spotted behind most of the houses along that street, so I guessed it had been a popular model here in Goldendale.

Inside the Potter house it was cool. There was a parlor to the left and on the right a dining room. A hallway with a telephone on the wall was smack in the middle. On one side of the hall was a corridor, which I guessed went to the kitchen. On the other side was a steep flight of stairs leading to the second story.

Mrs. Potter pointed to the parlor. Oh, that parlor of hers! Just one look into it would tell anybody how artistic she was. One whole wall was covered with blue and red prize ribbons. In the middle of the floor was a big quilting frame with a quilt she was working on fastened inside it. Everywhere I looked I saw baskets overflowing with things she was doing—knitting, crocheting, tatting, and embroidering. The back of every chair had a fancy antimacassar on it, and there were two or three doilies on each little table, when one would have been enough. In front of the bay window was another table stacked with white dishes, jars of paints, and paint brushes. So she was a china painter, too.

The room also had gold velvet drapes with fringes, a pink carpet, golden oak furniture, kerosene lamps, and one picture, the usual one of an Indian slumped over his horse, just like the one we had at home. There was a stereopticon slide viewer and a box of slides next to me. I hoped the slides would be some I hadn't seen. Sarah Jane and I edged our way past the quilting frame and sat down where we could find a seat, waiting for Mrs. Potter to return.

As we had come into the room, she had waved her hands and said she'd be gone for an instant only. She was true to her word and came right back, fluttering a long white envelope at Sarah Jane. My sister was trapped behind the quilting frame, so I got up to get the envelope and handed it to her.

Of course, it had to be Edgar's letter. I watched Sarah Jane clasp it to her chest with a sigh, then turn it over and look at the back. She muttered, "He wrote SWAK on it. Isn't that sweet of him?"

"Swak? That sounds terrible."

"Be pleasant, Melinda. It means sealed with a kiss."

Mush! I didn't say a word. I picked up the box of slides while she opened the letter and started to read. She didn't get too far before she said, "Melinda, his handwriting is simply dreadful. This is very hard going. It reminds me of chicken tracks I saw once in the mud after a rain."

"Does he say anything that isn't mushy?"

"I think he's writing about the house he rented for us in San Francisco. I think I can make out the words *sink* and *ice box* and *bathtub*. It's getting worse. It starts going uphill, then it goes downhill. Oh, well, perhaps his handwriting will improve later on in the letter when he's warmed it up a bit."

As I rummaged through the slides, I heard her muttering aloud the words of the letter as she tried to figure them out. Then all at once she let out a gasp and cried out, "Oh, Edgar!"

I figured she had got a whole big wad of mush and was

responding to it, so I got up to look at the wall of ribbons behind me. As I guessed, they were county-fair prizes for ladies' homecrafts.

Suddenly I heard Sarah Jane say, "It's off! It's all off between me and Edgar Everett Potter! Who does he think he is to write me such a thing?"

I whirled about to ask, "What's wrong?"

"Read his letter! Read it for yourself! Look at that last paragraph!" Oh, but Sarah Jane was mad, stamping her foot, her eyes flaming green and blue sparks of anger. I had never seen her so mad before in all my life.

I went around the frame, got the letter, and read the last paragraph out loud, struggling with the handwriting:

I must tell you how your loneliness has stricken me to the heart. There you stood next to my knight and his mount, and all I could see was your great loneliness. I am your knight in shining armor. I knew I would slay dragons for you the moment I set eyes on you. Many men would be afraid to wed someone so lonely as you, but not me. My heart was captured by your loneliness. I long to rescue you from Chicago and bring you to San Francisco. I long to make my lonely one happy. Now, my dearest lonely one, we will soon be together as husband and wife.

Lonely? What was he talking about? I stared at Sarah

Jane, who was biting her lips. Why would he think she was lonesome? After all, I'd been with her the day they'd met at the fair. And she'd had dozens of beaux and lots of girl friends, too. As far as I knew, she'd never been lonesome in her whole life.

Just then Mrs. Potter came back with a tray of ruby-red glasses and asked, "Sally, did you manage to make out Edgar's handwriting? It can be difficult sometimes."

My sister's voice was as tinkly cold sounding as the ice in the drink as she answered, "Oh, yes, I believe I managed to make out the important things your son wrote."

Mrs. Potter went on, "We ask Edgar to print when he writes to us, but he doesn't remember. He was never good at penmanship at school. Now take off your hats, and when my husband comes in we'll have a nice chat before supper. You'll be here three days, so we'll have enough time to talk. I want to hear all about how you two met and about his prune sculpture."

With her hand pressed to her forehead, Sarah Jane said, "Mrs. Potter, I don't want to talk about the prune horse and rider, and I don't want to talk about your son. Our engagement is broken as of four minutes ago."

Mrs. Potter put down the tray and asked, "What's wrong? Was it something he wrote in the letter?"

I said, "Yes, ma'am, it surely was. It's in the very last paragraph. Shall I show it to her, Sarah Jane?"

At my sister's nod, I gave the letter to Mrs. Potter, who stood and read aloud exactly what I had. Then she returned the letter to me and said, "That boy! He was always so kindhearted. He used to bring home wounded birds and little animals. He pities you because he sees you as lonesome and wants to save you. He should not have written this, of course, but he was always an honest boy, and it does show how tenderhearted he is."

"Honest!" cried Sarah Jane. "Brutally frank, I'd call him! I am *not* lonely. I have *never* been lonely." While Mrs. Potter gasped, she stamped her foot again. "I don't want to go to San Francisco to marry a man who pities me because he imagines I'm lonesome. And I don't want to go back to Chicago and be an object of pity to my family and all my friends." She turned to me. "Melinda, I never let on to you, but some of my friends warned me that I should not consider marrying a man I'd known for such a short time. They didn't like his sending me only short telegrams, and, frankly, neither did I. I kept looking for a letter. I'd rather die than go back home and admit they were right about him. I've never been lonesome, I've never been pitied, and I won't be pitied now! As for Edgar Everett Potter, I never want to see him again or speak to him or write him or telegraph him."

Oh, what a mess! I sighed. If I'd been my sister, I would have got on the next train for Chicago and told everybody what sort of crazy galoot Edgar Potter was and how glad I was that I'd found out before I'd married him. And I'd have written him a letter that would let him know just how much I wanted his pity!

While Sarah Jane fumed, I asked Mrs. Potter, "Does your son drink, maybe?"

"Not that I know of. Edgar always was a fine boy. Oh, I hate to see you hurt, Sally. I hate to see Edgar wounded. He's—"

She would have gone on praising him, but her husband came in the back way, struggling with our suitcases. He dropped them and said, puffing, "What's the trouble here? You all look like you just heard the Civil War had started up again."

I handed him his son's letter and said, "Read the last paragraph, Mr. Potter."

He read it to himself, then handed it back to me, saying, "Marrying somebody just because they happen to look lonesome is a big mistake. I thought the boy had better sense. He shouldn't have told your sis what he really thinks of her either."

Because he was looking at me, I answered, "No, he shouldn't have. Mr. Potter, Sarah Jane says that the engagement's off and she won't go on to Frisco. She won't go home either, so I guess we are going to stay here for a time."

He sighed and said, "I can't say as I blame her for not going out to Edgar after this. Marriage is a thing a person ought to be danged sure about before he or she takes the big leap."

"I will not be pitied in Chicago!" said my sister.

He nodded. "Yep, pity's a hard thing to bear up under. All right, stay here in Goldendale with us a while and do some deep thinking."

"No, I will not stay in this house!" flared Sarah Jane. "Is there a hotel?"

"Sure there is," I told her. "We passed some in town." When Sarah Jane didn't say anything more, I decided I had better take a hand, so I asked Mr. Potter, "Would you take us to a hotel?"

"Sure, I will. I'll hitch up the team and take your baggage out again." He shook his head. "Edgar'll be expecting Sally in Frisco."

I said, "We'll send him a telegram saying she isn't coming. He likes telegrams. Should I do that for you, Sarah Jane?" I asked my sister.

She didn't answer me. She only nodded. That meant I was to take a hand, all right. Before I did, though, I asked one more time, "Are you absolutely sure you don't want to go to either San Francisco or Chicago?"

"I am absolutely sure, Melinda. I've never been more sure of anything in my life! Send a telegram to him and say whatever you want, but make sure you tell him not to expect me—*ever!*"

3
The Judge

So Mr. Potter hitched up the team again, brought it to the front of the house, and loaded us and our suitcases into it. His wife stayed behind, looking upset and crying into her handkerchief.

He drove us into Goldendale again, and got us a room at the Pronghorn Hotel. Sarah Jane marched straight up the steps to our room without saying a word to either one of us. I figured she might be about to cry and wanted to be alone.

After Mr. Potter had gone on his way and I'd seen the hotel boy carry our baggage up to the room, I walked down to the telegraph station on the railroad platform.

I sent two telegrams for Sarah Jane, although I signed my name to them. To Edgar I wrote: "Sister eloped with a train conductor coming here. Forget her."

To Aunt Rhoda and Uncle Julius I wired: "Edgar drowned recently San Francisco Bay. Sarah Jane grieving here."

Those two messages would give Sarah Jane time to rest up in Goldendale, and keep Edgar in San Francisco and our relations at home in Chicago. Naturally, I'd write to Chicago right away and tell our aunt and uncle the real story. I was pretty sure that the Potters wouldn't write or telegraph their son about Sarah Jane's reaction to his letter. Besides, they knew I planned to telegraph him for Sarah Jane myself.

Feeling noble about having taken a hand for the Carpenter family, I went back to the hotel and up to our room. Sarah Jane was lying on the bed with a cold cloth over her forehead. That meant she had a headache. I told her, "I sent two telegrams for you, Sarah Jane."

"Thank you, Melinda," she said faintly, then added, "I want to try to sleep. Why don't you go down to dinner here? I can't eat."

Dinner suited me just fine. I was hungry enough to eat half a cow. I looked at Sarah Jane just before I left and saw that there were tears coming from under the cloth. She wasn't just mad, she was sad, too. Dang that Edgar Everett Potter!

Because the dining room of the Pronghorn Hotel had white tablecloths and napkins like Chicago cafes, I figured the food would be good. It was. So was the service. The middle-aged, redheaded waitress who took my order for roasted chicken didn't ask me first if I could pay for it or where my papa or mama were. She brought me my food fast and it was fine.

I was looking forward to maple pudding for dessert when suddenly Abraham Lincoln walked into the dining room and sat down at the table across from mine. He was very tall, bearded, dark and sad-looking, dressed all in black with a white shirt and black string tie. While I gawked at him, he looked at me, nodded in a natural way, and picked up the menu card on the table. Lincoln nodding to me? No, it couldn't be. He'd been killed twenty-eight years ago and buried in Illinois. He couldn't be sitting down to order dinner in Colorado, but he was! I couldn't eat another bite. All I could do was stare at him.

After a while the waitress came over, smiled at me, patted me on the shoulder, and sashayed over to Lincoln as if it was something she did all the time.

She said clear as could be, "Well, the soup's not so good tonight, but I can recommend the boiled dinner, Judge."

The man's voice was deep and like a bell, the way I figured Mr. Lincoln's should be. "All right, Clara, make it the boiled dinner tonight."

It wasn't Abe Lincoln. I knew that for sure. If he

ordered a boiled dinner, it had to be a real, live man. As the waitress wrote down his order, she asked him, "How's Edward Gideon been today, Judge? I haven't seen hide nor hair of the big scamp."

"He doesn't change, Clara. He's a sore trial to me. Let me ask you again. Will you change your mind about keeping house for him and me?"

"No, sir. I like it where I am. I'm part owner here and I'm too old to deal much with the likes of Edward Gideon. What do you want for dessert tonight, the usual?"

"Yes, the apple pie, as always. Will you please bring me my coffee and the evening paper now?"

"Sure thing." I saw her take a newspaper off a nearby table and put it beside his plate. He opened it and began to read as she left for the kitchen. I started eating again, but not for long. The man put down his paper and said to me, "Little lady, I've just now read about the man who started over Niagara Falls on a three-quarter-inch-wire cable, carrying a cookstove with him. He set it down on the wire, lit a fire in it, and then carried the whole thing to the other side."

I told him, "That story was in the Chicago paper I read on the train my sister and me came on to Goldendale. Chicago's our hometown." I added, "In that same paper I also read about a lion that escaped from its cage at the zoo in Philadelphia and would have got away except for a helpful elephant that grabbed the lion with his trunk, threw him to the ground, and put his foot on him till the keepers got there."

"Now, that is most interesting! I had not thought Philadelphia would have such goings-on. I am very interested in animal life. The Goldendale paper doesn't seem to go in much for items like that. I'm Judge Jedediah Garway. Who would you be, miss?"

"Melinda Albertine Carpenter." How well the judge talked! I said, "My big sister's named Sarah Jane. She's upstairs with a headache."

"Will you two be staying long?"

"It all depends on what she decides."

"Well, I hope you will enjoy your stay in Goldendale."

I said, "I doubt if we'll be here very long. Did the Goldendale paper have the story about the knight on horseback made out of California prunes for our Chicago fair? It's because of that sculpture that we're here in Goldendale at all. . . ." I would have gone on, but just then the waitress came in and plunked the judge's boiled dinner down in front of him.

She told him, "Eat it while it's hot. When it cools off, it tastes as bad as it looks." To me she said, "Your pudding's coming right up."

After she'd gone, the judge told me, "Clara takes good care of me. Maybe if you stay, we'll talk some more later on."

I nodded and when my pudding came ate it in silence. After I finished, I nodded at the judge again, buttered two biscuits I hadn't eaten and wrapped them in a napkin, dropped them into the pocket of my Eton suit, and went up to our hotel room.

Sarah Jane was sleeping, so I tiptoed over to a chair beside the open window and sat down to look out onto the main street of Goldendale. Where Chicago had street-lights in some parts of town, there weren't even gaslights here yet. The only thing lighting the street was the full moon. It made the dirt of the road silvery gold and sort of pretty. How fresh the air smelled! I could hear fast ragtime piano music that must have come from the nearest of the nine saloons, but that was the only noise. It was very peaceful.

Then I heard voices from below. One of them was the judge's deep one. The other was a man's, too, but higher. After a time I saw them crossing the street together. The shorter man was smoking a cheroot that glowed red on the end. I heard him say, "The price of silver's down to seventy-two cents an ounce. That's not good for Colorado and Goldendale."

"No, Mr. Mayor, it isn't, but the farmers and the mines are going to keep us going. There are some schemes afoot and we've got a number of advantages with the legislature. Of course, as you were saying in the lobby, things would be better for Goldendale if we get the county seat once the county is split up into two parts. The state capital will have to make a decision about the county seat ere long. Well, I'm headed for the Bonanza Palace Saloon to see if Edward Gideon's in there again. That's where I found him last night when I went out to hunt him down. The people there were feeding him hard-boiled eggs. He was so . . ."

The last I heard as the two men passed out of earshot was the mayor chuckling. I thought that was sure heartless of him. I pitied the judge. He must have a drunkard for a son.

A wan-looking Sarah Jane came down to breakfast with me. I could see that she was still upset. She didn't even ask what I'd said in the telegrams. She wouldn't take anything but toast and coffee. When I ordered stewed prunes, my sister gave me a wicked look and hissed at me. "Melinda, how can you remind me of him so soon?" She sighed. "How could I ever have thought I loved him! I must have gone crazy. I will never again eat a prune. I've been doing some thinking. From now on Chicago will be full of bad memories. I think I will go to New York City and find work as a lady salesclerk or a telephone-company operator or study to become a typewriter girl."

New York? I'd never seen it, either. I asked eagerly, "How about me? What'll I do there?"

"Nothing. You're too young to go. I'll be lonely there and I'll miss you, but you must go home to Chicago and finish your schooling there. It's still your home, but I can't think of it as mine anymore."

I said, "But it's your home, too!"

"No, Melinda, no! As soon as I finish my toast, I'm going to see about trains going east."

She headed for the depot, and I headed for our hotel room, where I found the horrible yellow tag in one of her suitcases and tore it to bits before we'd have a big argument about my wearing it. Then I came down again and sat in a chair on the hotel's porch to wait for Sarah Jane.

Goldendale was wide awake. There were people on the wooden sidewalks, and rigs and wagons in the street. There were also kids my age and younger, all going in the same direction on their way to school. Some looked happy. Others looked glum, which was like Chicago. I moved to the front of the porch and sat in a rocker, thinking with joy of the classes in choral music and the solo singing I was missing.

The Goldendale kids who passed were curious about me. I stuck out like a sore thumb because I wasn't in school. A yellow-haired girl in a white dress came out of a store next to the hotel. She stared at me as she went by, then hurried on ahead to catch up to a girl with long, red braids who was walking down the middle of the street. A big, black-haired boy in blue-and-white-striped bib overalls went past with two other big boys. Oh, how he stared at me! I felt like sticking my tongue out at him because I don't like being gawked at, but before I could do anything, another boy punched him in the ribs and said, "Come on, Stump! It's only a girl." What a name! Stump!

I figured part of the attention I was getting was due to the way I was dressed. My white Eton suit, straw hat with blue ribbons, and white high-top shoes were fine for Chicago. But girls in Goldendale wore cotton pinafores and black shoes.

At last, all the children had passed by, and I was alone, listening to the ringing of the school bell, waiting for Sarah Jane. She was sure taking her time at the train station.

Finally I saw her walking very slowly along the opposite side of the street. When she crossed over to me, the look on her face wasn't comforting. She didn't look as angry now as she had yesterday afternoon, but rather sad and beaten down. With a sigh, she sat down next to me and said, "Melinda, I just found out that I haven't got enough money to buy a ticket to New York. For that matter, there's not enough money to get me back to Chicago. Since I had expected to stay out in California,

my ticket was only one-way. Even if we both turn in our
fares for the rest of the way to California, we haven't got
enough money to buy me a ticket east."

"But you've got Uncle Julius's wedding-present check,
haven't you?"

"Yes, but I can't cash it because it's made out to Sarah
Jane *Potter,* not Carpenter."

"What'll we do, Sarah Jane?"

"I've been thinking about that. I'm afraid you'll have
to go back to Chicago alone on the return ticket you
have. I'll stay here in Goldendale and find a job. Once I've
saved enough money, I'll go on to New York."

I leaped up. *"No!* If you stay, I'll stay, too. That's what
our relatives would want. They wanted me to go to
California with you, so they'll want me to stay here with
you! Don't worry about me missing school. I can go to
the one here in Goldendale."

Sarah Jane sighed. "Oh, I suppose you could . . . for
a while anyhow." She touched my knee as I sat down
again. "Thank you, Melinda, for your loyalty. Well,
now, what can I do to earn a living here? After I inquired
about tickets at the depot, I went to the newspaper office
and looked at the help-wanted ads. Somebody wants a
milliner, but I can't trim hats. Another wants a typewriter
girl. There were very few ads asking for ladies."

Remembering what the mayor and judge had said, I
answered, "Jobs are scarce here, I bet. Times aren't so

good. The price of silver is only seventy-two cents an ounce, and this isn't the county seat."

"What are you talking about, Melinda?" Sarah Jane sounded cross.

I said, "Nothing much. It was only something I overheard last night. Weren't there any other jobs?"

"Just one, as housekeeper and cook to a Judge something or other."

"Was it a Judge Garway?"

"Why, yes, I think that was the name." She was staring at me. "How did you know that?"

"I met him last night at supper. He eats here at the hotel. He talked to me."

"Melinda, you should not talk to strange men."

"He isn't strange. He isn't one bit of a masher. He's sort of different, but I think he's harmless. The way he looks, he's got to be a good man. Besides, Uncle Julius says all judges are very respectable, even the Republican ones. I think I'll go inside and find out some more about the judge. The waitress knows him real good, I think."

"Oh, Melinda," exclaimed Sarah Jane, shaking her head, but she didn't try to stop me.

I got up, shook out my skirt, pulled up my long, white stockings, and, looking presentable, went inside.

Clara, the waitress, was setting the tables for lunch in the dining room, and I went over and asked if I could speak with her alone. After we talked for a few minutes, she took me out to the kitchen, past the Chinese cook, and opened the back door onto the alley behind the hotel.

"That's Edward Gideon. You asked about him and there he is. The lazy good-for-nothing comes here in the mornings for a handout and falls asleep on the mat."

I gasped with surprise. There, draped across the door-mat, hanging over it in all directions, was the biggest, most gangling black dog I'd ever seen in my entire life. The Great Dane was snoring, sound asleep. A gnawed beef bone lay on the ground beside him.

After I'd seen and heard enough, we went back through the kitchen to the dining room, and Clara went on with her work. I went out onto the porch, sat beside Sarah Jane, and said, "I talked to Clara, who's known Judge Garway for years. She says he's a prince of a fellow. His sister kept house for him but died last year, and now he needs a housekeeper. She says he's got a nice house and a nice nature, and if she didn't own part of this hotel she'd go to work for him herself. When I asked if the judge's son, Edward Gideon Garway, was a drunkard, she showed me that he wasn't."

"What are you talking about, Melinda? Who is that?"

"Edward Gideon. He's a bum, but not a drunkard. She showed me where he fell asleep on the mat outside the kitchen door after he was fed."

"Asleep on the doormat?"

"That's right, dead to the world. I wonder how many boiled eggs he ate last night at the saloon. I guess the judge never did catch him, or maybe he got loose early this morning."

"What is all this, Melinda Carpenter?"

So now I told her all about the judge and his dog, about my talk with the judge himself, and how much I had taken to him.

Sarah Jane said, "Oh, how exasperating children your age can be! So you and the waitress think I ought to go to work for this man I've never seen? I have no idea at all what he plans to pay a housekeeper and cook, you know."

I said, "The waitress said he's a big tipper here," and reached out to pat my sister's hand soothingly. "Let me take a hand, Sarah Jane, to help us out. All you have to do is come to supper in the dining room with me tonight, and I'll get you a job offer. After all, I sent the telegrams for you, didn't I?"

Sarah Jane sank down in her chair, frowning. Then she asked, "By the way, what did you put in them?"

When I told her, she looked astonished. Then she smiled for the first time in hours. She didn't say anything but, "We'll have to clear that fib up with Aunt Rhoda and Uncle Julius soon, of course, but why not let Edgar believe I found a man I met on a train more attractive than he is! I doubt if I would have sent that message, but yours will keep him in California—and that's exactly where I want him to be."

We two were halfway through our supper when the judge came into the dining room. Naturally, I watched my sister's face to see what she thought about seeing Abe Lincoln. How she stared. He sort of bowed to her and me, then went to the same table as the night before. After ordering fried chicken, he took up the Goldendale paper.

Before he could start reading, I asked him, "Did you read about the famous milk-cow race from Texas to the Chicago fair, Judge?"

He put down the paper and said, "No, I guess the *Goldendale Press* didn't carry that information."

I said, "Well, it was some race, wasn't it, Sarah Jane?"

"I don't know. I never heard of it." Sarah Jane was still staring at Judge Garway.

I went on. "Well, Sarah Jane, you've had other things on your mind lately because you lost your job as a housekeeper to the artist in Chicago who makes sculptures out of fruits for the fair. You're worried about getting another job as a housekeeper somewhere because that's the only kind of work you can really do, though you're surely good at that." I took a deep breath and went on. "Well, Judge, I do keep telling her not to trust artists. Anyhow, to get back to the cow race. First prize was a whole five thousand dollars, which in my view is too much money as a prize for gambling. Any man in Texas who wanted to race could enter his cow. Each contestant was given a two-wheeled buggy, pots and pans, a hundred pounds of meat, fifty pounds of bacon, ten pounds of coffee, and one butter churn. The men and their milk cows had to travel twelve hours a day north to Chicago, and when they stopped for the night, each man had to milk the cow and churn her milk into butter. The person that made it with his cow to Chicago with the most butter in the churn won the five thousand dollar prize, but there had to be at least fifty pounds of butter in it by then or he didn't qualify. The butter must have been pretty bad by that time."

I finished and waited, watching Judge Garway as he stared at my sister. I'd taken a hand for her again, and my plot was working. He'd been interested in both of my stories, but was a lot more excited by the one about her being a housekeeper.

He asked her, "Miss Carpenter, did I hear correctly that you are looking for employment as a housekeeper?"

Before she could say "Not really" or "I'm not sure," I kicked her gently under the table and said, "Yes, she is. Me, too. I can run errands and help out in the house. I can also feed chickens and gather eggs."

Now he looked at me and said, "I have no hens, but I have a dog, a rather unusual canine. How are you with dogs, little lady?"

"Fine, just fine, so long as they aren't the little, tiny, yapping kind."

Judge Garway smiled. "My dog is not small and not a yapper. All right, ladies, I would be honored if you would come back to my house with me after supper. If you two like my home, we can then discuss financial matters. You will not find me ungenerous, Miss Carpenter."

"All right, sir," replied Sarah Jane. She didn't sound very enthused since the only housekeeping she'd done before was to help Aunt Rhoda with the chores. Yet I knew she'd caught the words *not ungenerous,* because she'd kicked me back under the table when he'd spoken them.

As for me, I was already composing my next telegram to Aunt Rhoda and Uncle Julius: "Both staying, comforting Potters. Working, housekeeping for judge and dog."

❦4❧
Doubts!

The judge's house was just like the Potters', model 42-A, although it wasn't as cluttered up with handicrafts. It was neat but dusty. I was comforted to see that there were no spittoons, which told me the judge wasn't a tobacco chewer. There was no job worse than cleaning out spittoons.

After looking into cupboards and closets the judge held open for her, Sarah Jane told him, "All right, I'll keep house for you. Melinda and I will move in in the morning. I'll need some money to buy food, because you haven't got many supplies in your kitchen. I saw that your flour bin's full of weevils, and you're out of sugar and coffee beans."

The judge beamed as he told her, "No, I don't keep supplies anymore. I eat out from necessity. I'll give you whatever money you require for foodstuffs, Miss Carpenter, plus sixty dollars per month wages. That's generous pay for these hard financial times. You two will have the two rooms over the front porch. One more thing—you won't have to worry about my laundry. I send everything to a Chinese laundryman."

Sarah Jane nodded and said, "Sixty dollars is fine, sir. What will you be paying Melinda?"

As I held my breath, he leaned against the hallway wall next to the telephone and said, "A dime every time she fetches my dog back here to the yard. Now, come back through the house and I'll show you that, too."

I went happily. A dime was good pay!

We went out through the kitchen and screened-off porch to the fenced-in backyard. There stood Edward Gideon a distance away under the clotheslines, looking at us as if he'd never seen ladies before. He didn't growl or bark or wag his tail. He only looked.

"Does he bite?" asked Sarah Jane.

The judge said, "No, he is peaceable by nature, though he's greatly given to wanderlust." As the dog started to twitch, the judge suddenly shouted, "Stay, boy, stay!"

I watched Edward Gideon lumber toward the board fence, gather his long, black legs under him, and leap. He landed on top of the fence, hung there teetering, and slid down the other side.

Sarah Jane exclaimed, "Good heavens, the fence is taller than he is! It must be nearly as tall as Melinda."

The judge said, "If I'd had it built any taller it would rankle my neighbors. I dare not do that since they say they vote for me. As it is, it's the tallest fence in town, but it does not hold an animal of his size and strength and spirit, as you see."

My sister asked, "Why didn't you tie him up?"

"He chews through any rope I buy. I cannot chain him and break his spirit. He's a young dog for all his size." Judge Garway sighed. "I don't want him to run free and perhaps become the sire of a litter of half-breed puppies. Nor do I want him to be involved in dog fights, which could involve me in lawsuits. I'm torn about him. My sister, God rest her, didn't want his spirit trammeled. She liked spirit in man and beast. She was willing to hunt him down and so am I, though she had more time for that. She tracked him until her health failed."

I thought it was noble of the judge not to chain Edward Gideon. What's more, his not doing it gave me a job. But there was still a problem. I told the judge, "I have to go to school, so I can't be your dog tracker except before and after school and on weekends. Could I maybe chain him outside the schoolhouse while I'm inside?"

"No, he howls when he's tied anywhere. The neighbors here complain. I have tried to chain him temporarily while I'm inside the city hall holding court. The mayor and the attorneys complain then. A dog that size has a mighty howl. Your teacher would never permit you to do that.

"It may seem odd to you and your sister, but I want Edward Gideon here at least some of the time. I hope to curb some of his wanderlust and to get him to realize that he belongs here. I keep hoping someday he will stay of his own accord with his spirit unbroken. You will simply have to hunt him down before and after school and bring him home on a leash. You can attach it to his collar."

I said, "Yes, sir, I saw the collar. It's leather and looks to be danged strong."

"It is, child. I had the blacksmith make it for him. It has to be strong."

Early the next morning, a friend of the judge's drove us and our suitcases to the Garway house on Cedar Street. We passed the same two girls that I'd seen yesterday on their way to school. We all stared some more. This time, because they would soon be part of my life here, I grinned at them. Then I glared at the boys walking behind them. There was no reason not to be prepared at the new school I'd be starting tomorrow morning.

The judge wasn't home, but his front door was un-locked, so we opened it and went inside. I unpacked in my little room with the yellow-rosebud paper on the walls. Because I had only one suitcase it didn't take me long. Then I went downstairs to find Edward Gideon. The waitress at the hotel had given me meat scraps for him that morning. But he wasn't there to eat them. I set the food beside his water dish and went back to sit on the front steps and wait for Sarah Jane to come down.

Judge Garway's house wasn't far from Main Street. From where I sat, I could see horses and buggies and wagons passing along it. As I leaned my head in my hands, I spied Mr. Potter's wagon. I jumped up and ran down the street toward him. Mr. Potter saw me and reined in his team. Now I saw that he wasn't alone. He had one of those English brothers, Mr. Alfred, with him.

"Good morning, Melinda," said Mr. Potter. He was very calm about things.

After saying "Good morning" back to him, I told him, "I haven't got time to talk long, but my sister and I are staying on here for a while working for Judge Garway. Please tell your wife that we're still in Goldendale and not to mention your son's name to my sister if she ever sees us. We haven't got anything against you two, just against him. If you write to him, please don't let him know Sarah Jane's here. I have to get back to her now. Good-bye."

I didn't really wait to hear what Mr. Potter would say. I thought he was muttering something under his breath, but I could sure hear the Englishman, whose voice cut through a person like a hot knife through butter. "My word, Potter, who was that odd child? Wasn't she accompanying that handsome gel I saw with your wife on the railroad platform the other day? Am I correct in assuming that the betrothal between your son and the gel is broken? Well, well, she's bound to be the toast of Goldendale. . . ."

And that was all I heard before Mr. Potter started his team to trotting away.

Sarah Jane didn't say a single word when I told her later about my conversation with Mr. Potter. She only nodded. Nor did she smile when I told her that the Englishman thought she was pretty and had sounded pleased that she wasn't engaged to Edgar Everett anymore. Her mind was on the business of housekeeping, nothing else.

Armed with a twenty-dollar gold piece Judge Garway had left on the hall table for groceries, we hiked down to the store he had told Sarah Jane about, Mittelman's Emporium. He had said it was the best place to shop, and standing inside the store, looking around at all the hundreds of things in it, I agreed with him. It had canned food, horse collars, blankets, yard goods, thread, candles, seventy-five-cent corsets, chairs and stools, barrels of pickles and sauerkraut, saws, hoes, axes, lanterns—just about anything a body would need except for fresh meat, fish, and fresh bread. There were a lot of people working there. I saw a big man with a yellow beard and three younger men, two brown-haired and another redheaded with pink fuzz on his cheeks. There was a lady store clerk, too, tiny, with red-yellow hair and bright blue eyes. She sold us the red-and-blue cloth I needed for my school pinafores and aprons. She was very friendly toward us. After we'd done all our buying, she came out from behind the cloth counter to talk.

She told us her name was Huldah Mittelman. Then she motioned toward the four galoots and said, "They are my husband and sons."

When I told her that we were living at Judge Garway's house, she said, "Oh, he's a fine man. We've known him ever since my husband, Aaron, gave up being a wagon peddler and we settled down here to have our family."

I asked, "Does his dog come in here?"

She laughed and said, "Oh, yes. He makes his rounds and sometimes my Esther takes him back to the judge. Would you be in the eighth grade like my daughter?"

"Yes'm. I'm an eighth grader, and you'll be seeing me if Edward Gideon comes in here. Finding him is going to be my job. Do other kids take him back home?"

"Yes, the judge always gives them a dime when they do."

I nodded and said, "That's what he's paying me, too. Do you have any idea where the dog is right now?"

Mrs. Mittelman shook her head. "The saloons are your best bet."

Sarah Jane said now, "Melinda should not go inside

saloons. A boy could go in, but not a girl." She frowned. "I had not thought of saloons. I've had so much else on my mind . . ."

The lady storekeeper interrupted. "She won't have to go inside. She can go to the back door and call out the dog's name. Somebody will haul him out by the collar. Esther says the judge sometimes does that when he's in too much of a hurry to go in and have a drink."

I asked, "Will the dog come to a whistle?"

"Esther says he won't. Sometimes he'll come to his name—if he's of a mind to."

Sarah Jane uttered impatiently, "I never dreamed when I left Chicago a week ago that I'd ever be standing in a store in Colorado talking about getting a dog out of saloons. This dog seems to be a town character."

"So is Judge Garway." Mrs. Mittelman smiled, then snapped her fingers and added, "Wait a minute, please. His special tonic arrived in a shipment from Boston yesterday afternoon. I'll get it for you and add it to your bill." And she was gone.

"Do you suppose he's a sick man?" Sarah Jane asked me crossly.

After a time Mrs. Mittelman was back with a brown paper bag. She handed it to my sister with the words, "Whatever you do, don't drop this. It's all I have. Last time I saw the judge closeup in the full light of day he needed it. He was beginning to show. Give it to him right away."

"Is the judge ill?" asked Sarah Jane.

Mrs. Mittelman said, "I think you'd better ask him about his tonic yourself. He doesn't care to have people know about it."

Sarah Jane was nettled. I could tell by the brisk way she said, "All right. I'd better pay you and be on my way. I have work to do."

Mrs. Mittelman didn't seem to mind Sarah Jane's tone of voice. She smiled and said, "Of course, of course. I did enjoy our chat just now. I get to talk with women when they come in to buy yard goods and ladies' things." Her face darkened now. "But ladies don't come in for such merchandise every day, and I don't work on Saturdays when the country women come to town in wagons." She patted my arm and said, "Dear, I'm going to ask Esther to look out for you tomorrow on your first day of school. Some of the boys are rather rough. I hope you and Esther will be friends."

"I'm sure we will if she's as nice as you are."

"What a sweet thing to say."

As we left loaded down with bundles, Mrs. Mittelman came out onto the sidewalk to wave good-bye.

"I think she's lonesome," I told Sarah Jane under my breath.

My sister mumbled, "I think she was trying to tell me
the judge has hoodwinked me. I haven't started to work
for him yet, but already I have misgivings, Melinda. I
plan to have a talk with him tonight about a number of
things, including when we get our day off."

"Sarah Jane, what'll we do with a day off when we do
get it?"

"I don't know about you, Melinda, but I plan to lie
down in my room with the curtains drawn and think dark
thoughts about someone else who must be a town character along with the judge and his animal."

Suddenly I thought of something, set down my bundle,
and ran back to Mrs. Mittelman, who was just about to
go inside her store. I asked her, "If I call you on the
judge's telephone an ask if you've got his dog here, will
you hold him for me till I come for him?"

"If I'm in the store, yes, I'll try to hold him for you."

"Thanks. Would other folks hereabouts do that for
me?"

She shook her head. "I doubt it. They've got business
of their own to tend to. When the judge's dog takes a
notion to leave a place, they'd be inclined to let him have
his way."

"And the saloonkeepers?"

She waggled a finger at me. "Don't call them at all.
They'd probably laugh and hang up. Ladies are always
calling them asking for men who might be there. Thank

the Lord, my Aaron doesn't go to such places. Your sister wouldn't like you calling saloons." Mrs. Mittelman peered at me sharply. "Your sister is an unhappy young woman, isn't she? It sticks out all over her."

"Yes'm, right now she is. She just slipped a man a mitten and she's sad, but she'll get over it. She didn't know him for very long, so it wasn't like she really loved him."

"Wasn't it, my dear?" Mrs. Mittelman turned her head and I saw her husband in the doorway beckoning to her. She had to go inside and I had to catch up with Sarah Jane, who hadn't stopped.

I thanked her for her help and kindness, and off I ran to get my packages and catch up to my sister. When I did, I told her, "Sarah Jane, the Pronghorn Hotel's only a couple of doors from here. Would you wait outside while I look in the alley for Edward Gideon?"

"If he's there, Melinda, how do you plan to get him home?"

"With this." I took off the heavy cotton belt from my Eton suit. The skirt stayed up without it.

"All right, I'll wait for you. I suppose looking there now could save you looking there later."

That's where I found him, lolling all over the mat again, but awake this time. For a while I stood and stared at him, fixing him with my eye, remembering the judge had said he didn't bite. I hissed, "Edward Gideon, I am

Melinda Carpenter. I am your mistress. I work for your master. You are to come home with me now, this very minute. You will let me put this belt onto your collar."

He stood up, waiting. Holding my belt out for him to sniff, I came closer and closer, until I could tie it onto his collar. I let him get a good smell of me, the way Uncle Julius had taught me to do with dogs in Chicago. Then I gave a tug on the belt. Would he come with me?

Even sitting down, the Great Dane's head came up to my chest. His huge brown eyes looked up into mine. Neither of us blinked. All at once he got to his feet with a deep grumble. How big he was! Half a horse! I tugged again and now he moved a little. I could see what Mrs. Mittelman had meant when she had used the word *hauled*. Being paid a dime for each time I fetched this dog back home had sounded fine at the time, but by the way he was slowly slouching along behind me, I could see I might be earning every penny of it.

Five minutes later, as we headed for Cedar Street, that fresh, black-haired boy I'd seen the other day came bicycling toward us down Main Street. When he saw us he came rearing up onto the sidewalk, circled us on one wheel, and hooted at me, "Hey, are you walking the judge's dog or is he walking you?"

Edward Gideon refused to move at all now. He let out a bark, then a growl, and I saw his neck hairs bristling. I cried, "Run for your life or I'll sic him on you."

"All right, all right, call off your mutt," said the boy, and he rode off.

I looked at Edward Gideon, whose neck hairs had flattened down a bit. I told Sarah Jane, "We just learned something. He either doesn't like bicycles or he doesn't like boys. He sure doesn't like that one, and neither do I. Which one do you think it is, Sarah Jane?"

"Melinda, don't mention men to me. I don't know. I don't care. All I want to do is get to Cedar Street before these packages get so heavy I can't go another step with them."

Now I looked at my sister. Her hair was falling down in long, yellow tendrils. Her big straw sailor hat was askew, and there were tears on her flushed cheeks. I asked, "Are you awfully sad?"

"No, I'm mad, Melinda! I'm mad enough to spit nails out in the shape of a heart. Now, let's get that animal where we're going and hope he'll stay put for a time. I will not allow you to go out looking for him more than once a day. That dog could become a person's life work." She puffed air now, pushing with her lower lip, to get a tendril out of her eyes. She said, "I'd planned to stop at a butcher's and buy meat for supper, but I think I'd better make an omelet for the judge. Omelets are easy to digest. I'm going to talk with him tonight about this special tonic of his. I want to know why he sends all the way to Boston for it. I took a job as a housekeeper, not as a nurse."

"Judge Garway ate a boiled dinner and a chicken one at the hotel, but I never did see him eat red meat. That's all Uncle Julius will ever look at. I guess you'd better talk with him about his tonic." What had we got ourselves into?

Judge Garway didn't seem to mind his omelet dinner. He pushed his empty plate away and said, "Now that was fine, fine home cooking. I like eggs. What's for dessert, Miss Carpenter?"

"Custard," said Sarah Jane.

"More eggs, huh, and more milk, too?" He sounded less contented now.

Sarah Jane said, "I'm told that's excellent fare for people who may have health problems."

I added, "It's what our Aunt Rhoda always fixes for Uncle Julius when he's dyspeptic."

The judge leaned down to pat Edward Gideon, who'd sat looking hopefully at him during dinner. Then he spoke to the dog. "Boy, these ladies seem to think I'm feeble and need coddling. I've read in the newspapers that the latest rage is candied chrysanthemums, but I wouldn't take to them. I wonder what they have in mind to feed me next. I do believe you had your taster set for a steak bone, and I know I had mine set for a T-bone steak or something to chew on and give my jaws exercise enough to hold a cheroot between my teeth." He lifted his black eyebrows. "Well, Miss Carpenter?" He spoke to Sarah Jane now.

She told him, "I am delighted to hear about your digestion. Do you have delicate health anywhere else, sir?"

"Not one bit of it. What makes you think I do?"

"Wait here a moment and I will show you." Sarah Jane got up from the dining-room table, went into the kitchen, and came back with the brown paper bag from Mittelman's store. "Mrs. Mittelman gave me this. She said it was your special tonic from Boston and that she could see when you needed it. She was quite secretive about it."

"My Boston tonic, eh?" The judge's eyes weren't Lincoln-sad now but merry, yet he said a horrible thing. "I must tell you that I am dying. I've been dying by inches for more than twenty years. I use the tonic to keep me going. Mrs. Mittelman, bless her, watches me to see if I seem to be needing its benefits. But let me tell you, I have yet to put a drop of it into my stomach." Now he chuckled.

When neither of us said a word, he went on, "That is correct. Not a drop goes into my stomach. It goes onto my head and beard. I was fortunate enough to be born with deep-set, dark eyes, but fate didn't follow through to give me dark hair. In truth, I am a strawberry blond. As my hair grows, my roots show up light in bright sunshine. I watch for that. So does Mrs. Mittelman. In order to point up my resemblance to our great old president, I dye monthly."

I gasped out, "Why?"

"To get votes. I am an elected judge, not an appointed one. Few people in this country would vote against a man who looks like Abe Lincoln. I am hoping to be elected as judge here again, after that to the governorship of Colorado, and then be chosen by the people of this state as a United States senator. Does that answer your question?"

"Yes, sir, you bet. Does anyone else know about it besides you and Mrs. Mittelman?"

"No one but her and the two of you. I would have told you in any event. Black hair dye makes a God-awful mess you would have to deal with. My sister deplored how it stained walls and towels, but she knew why I went to the trouble. I trust you will, too?"

Quickly Sarah Jane said, "Yes, sir. We won't tell anyone, will we, Melinda?" Her glance told me I'd better promise, and I did. Well, maybe I would write Aunt Rhoda about it. Chicago was a long, safe ways off.

The judge spoke to me now. "I was pleased to see Edward Gideon when I came home tonight. How did you keep him here?"

"I sat in the backyard with him till you got home. I'd brought him scraps from the hotel."

"Aha, he had food and company. Sometimes that will hold him."

I said, "Judge, I never took my eyes off him and he never took his off me. Say, does he hate boys, or is it bicycles that make him growl?"

"Bicycles, I think. When he was younger, he was run into by some local boys racing down Main Street. We've got the usual collection of graceless scamps here." Bicycles? I'd thought it might have been that boy, Stump.

As I cleared off the omelet plates, I thought about school tomorrow. I'd need a T-bone steak for supper to put strength back into me after that. I was pretty sure Stump was going to be a deadly foe. Well, I'd had foes among boys in Chicago. I wasn't going to bawl at night over the doings of menfolk the way Sarah Jane had done.

I hoped she'd get over Edgar Everett fast and look around Goldendale for a new beau. Maybe she'd look in the direction of the English honourables. I wondered how old Judge Garway was; he could be years younger than he looked. But, then, Sarah Jane hadn't acted one bit flirty with him.

5
Friends and Foes
and Firecrackers

I looked for Edward Gideon the next morning, and just as I had figured, he'd taken off over the fence. I folded up his leather leash and put it into the pocket of the dress I was wearing for later use. Finding him and fetching him back home wasn't the top thing I had to do today. School was!

Sarah Jane, as my next of kin, walked me to the schoolhouse through a bunch of staring kids waiting to go inside. I smiled at the redheaded girl with braids and the blond one, whom I figured to be Esther Mittelman because she looked so much like Mrs. Mittelman. They both smiled back at me. Stump was inside the one-room schoolhouse writing on the blackboard, "I won't be tardy and I won't play hooky anymore." I saw at a glance that he'd written the sentence a dozen times already. His penmanship was passable; that was all I could say for it. We glared at each other, then I curtseyed to the teacher, a tall, thin woman in a black taffeta dress. She wore black-rimmed spectacles and a black straw hat with white doves nestling together in the front.

After Sarah Jane introduced us as coming from Chicago, the teacher said, "I am Miss Hawkins, and I am in charge here. So you went to school in Chicago. Well, I suspect you were in a bigger school with several classrooms. You are in the eighth grade now? We shall very soon see if you are up to our eighth-grade standards, Melinda."

Sarah Jane said, "Melinda was an A student in everything at her school."

Being truthful I added, "Except in choral music. I can't sing."

Now Miss Hawkins gave us a small smile. "No matter. We are scarcely large enough to have choral music here. I do not teach *everything*. I draw the line at choral music." She led the way to a back-row desk for two and said, "You will share this with Violet Stowe, the redheaded girl outside. I am moving Violet because she and Esther Mittelman whisper together too much. I trust you will not whisper, Melinda?"

"No, ma'am, not me."

I sat down and Sarah Jane left. Miss Hawkins walked out behind her with the school bell in her hand.

Violet Stowe soon slipped in beside me. I guessed Miss
Hawkins must have told her to outside. The blond girl
sat at her desk just across the aisle. She smiled and whispered quickly while the younger children were making
noise as they sat down, "I'm Esther Mittelman. Mama
told me your name." Then she fell quiet during the bell
ringing. I looked over the schoolhouse where I'd be
spending hours of my life from now on. It had black-
boards on two sides, a wood stove in one corner, rows of
double desks, the teacher's desk and chair, and two windows. That was all there was to it. No, this sure wasn't
like my two-story brick schoolhouse in Chicago. I felt
crowded here.

I also was nervous, and what I did for the next hour
and a half before morning recess didn't help any. Miss
Hawkins made me stand up and recite the whole multi-
plication table up to the twelves, then do long division
and fractions on the blackboard. After that, I had to read
aloud and come back to the board to show I could do
Spencerian handwriting. Finally, Miss Hawkins said that
I was worthy of her eighth grade. I went back wearily
to the desk and settled onto the bench beside Violet. She
grabbed my hand and squeezed it while Esther smiled at
me. I was among friends, and how fast it had happened!

At recess I went outside with Violet and Esther. They
asked me a lot of questions about Chicago and my old

school and about how long Sarah Jane and I would be in Goldendale. I told them all about us, but not what had brought us to Colorado. Later on, when I got to know them better, I might tell them about Edgar Everett Potter III, but not right now.

I told Esther, "I met your mother yesterday. It's sure nice of her to ask you to be my friend right away when you hardly know me yet. You two are the friendliest people I've ever run into."

Esther came closer to tell me, "Yes, we are friendly. This is Colorado. It's a friendly place. We decided to become friends with you partly because of Mama's taking to you and your sister, but there's another reason, Melinda Carpenter."

"Another one? What's that?"

Violet's green eyes darkened as she hissed, "Stump Wood said that he sure hated the new yellow-headed girl in town who was such a fancy dresser. He said she wanted to sic dogs on him. Anybody who is an enemy of Stump is a pal of mine and Esther's. Give me your hand, Melinda."

I shook hands with Violet, then with Esther. We went on talking about Miss Hawkins and her likes and dislikes until she rang the handbell ending recess. As we went back into the schoolhouse, I asked my friends, "Will you help me track down the judge's Great Dane sometimes? I'll give you some of the money I earn if you do."

Esther said, "Sure I will, but I won't take any money for it. Helping you would be a *mitzvah.*"

"What's that?"

Violet replied, "That's what she calls a good deed." After she thought for a moment, she said, "My mama says we ought to help others when we can. All right, I won't take any money from you either, then."

Now I asked, "Will you help me look for Edward Gideon today?"

Esther looked at Violet and said, "I guess I could. My violin lesson's tomorrow."

Violet frowned, then said, "Well, all right. I don't have to look after my baby brother today. It's my big sister's turn."

I rejoiced. Since they'd gone out after the dog before, they would know the places he'd likely be. And I'd have company while I was tracking him down, too. Even if things hadn't gone right for Sarah Jane here, they were for me.

After recess I had to give an oral report on the Chicago fair. It was fun, and how the kids laughed when I told them about the prune horse from California. I didn't tell them about the sculptor, though, because they might know him personally.

As I gave my report, I looked around the classroom at my schoolmates. One look at Stump's face told me he was a teaser. There were some bullies, too. I could spot them by sight right off. Two of them, with brown, bushy hair and freckly faces, sat in a desk in the last row and stuck their big boots out into the aisle. While I gave my report, they stared at me and didn't smile once. Miss Hawkins kept glancing their way, then back to me and the other kids in the room. She was a teacher who knew her onions. She'd be ready for anything and wouldn't put up with nonsense. That was the best kind of teacher to have—so long as a pupil behaved.

During lunch Esther and Violet told me quite a bit about Goldendale. While I chewed on the stringy corned-beef sandwich Sarah Jane had fixed for me, I heard all about Judge Garway. I knew some of it already—that he was an elected judge who had big plans for the future, and that he had lost his sister last year. But they also told me something interesting that was new to me. It seems he'd wanted the people of Goldendale to vote for tax money to build both a courthouse and a city hall this year. But because the times were not good at all, they only voted for a prefabricated city hall, which had been ordered and erected last spring. The judge was cramped for room there and was letting folks know about it. He was threatening to hold court in the Bonanza Palace, the biggest saloon in town, and according to Violet's papa, by law the judge could hold court wherever he wanted to.

Esther said, "Being cramped isn't his only trouble. My

papa says that the county we live in is too big and it's soon
going to be split up into two counties, west and east. The
western part doesn't matter to the Goldendale folks, but
the eastern half does."

I asked, "Why's that?"

Frowning, she explained, "Goldendale and Heberville
are the two biggest towns in the eastern half. One of them
will be the new county seat. It's important to be a county
seat because lots of folks come there on legal business.
They buy what supplies they need for the week or the
month at the same time. We want Goldendale to be
chosen. Judge Garway wants that, too, so he can be the
top judge in the county seat, courthouse or no courthouse."

I mumbled, "Is that so?"

Violet answered me, "It is so. The folks in Heberville
want their town to be the county seat. They voted to
build a city hall *and* a courthouse. It gets the judge's goat
that they have one."

I wasn't sure that I'd understood all they'd told me, but
I'd ponder on it later. All the same, I'd got a real earful
to tell Sarah Jane, and now I understood what I'd overheard from our hotel room the first night I'd met Judge
Garway.

The afternoon went by quickly, and after school the
three of us went off together to hunt for the judge's dog.
Stump and some of the other boys hooted at us, but we

wouldn't even look in their direction as we headed down Main Street for the Pronghorn Hotel, one of Edward Gideon's favorite places.

He wasn't there today. Neither was he inside any of the saloons. We tried the Mittelman Emporium, where I met Esther's brothers, Ben, Sam, and Joshua; but Mrs. Mittelman didn't have Edward Gideon either. We then walked to Violet's pa's blacksmith shop because the dog sometimes went there for handouts. I met her father and oldest brother, and learned that the dog hadn't come there.

Next we went to Violet's house. Her mama, older sister, and new baby brother were home, but not Edward Gideon. We had no luck at the fire station, the city hall, the barber shop, or undertaker, either. We even peeked into the pool hall where ladies never entered. No dog anywhere! Finally we all stood together on the boardwalk and asked ourselves where else he could be. Could he, glory be, have gone back to his own house?

Esther said, "No, he doesn't do that." She was biting on a ragged fingernail as she said, "You know, there is one other place he could be. Sometimes he goes over to visit Mrs. Dotty Potter. She bakes cookies for him that have meat in them. Sometimes she draws pictures of him."

I asked cautiously, "Dotty Potter?"

Violet said, "Oh, sure, the lady who lives on Elm Street. She wins all the county-fair prizes for being so artistic in everything."

Well, I guessed I knew who that was. I thought hard, then said, "Yes, I've met her already. My sister used to know a relative of hers in Chicago. He was artistic, too. He's called Edgar Everett. Do you know him?"

To my relief, both of my new friends shook their heads no. Violet said, "I heard the Potters had a son, but he's grown up and had gone away a long time ago. I never met him."

I told them, "He went all the way out to California. Well, let's go see if Mrs. Potter has Edward Gideon. Say, would somebody steal him?"

Esther said, "No, he's too big to hide."

"But maybe somebody who lives in the mountains or on the prairie dognapped him."

Violet told me, "No, if anybody took Edward Gideon, he wouldn't stay. He's a roamer by nature."

As we walked along in the dust, I said, "I'm not. I don't plan to make dogcatching my life's work. I think I want to be a high school teacher. Violet, what do you want to be?"

"I don't know yet, Melinda. Maybe a hat maker or a seamstress. Esther has great big plans, though."

"What are they?"

Esther smiled. "A secret, that's what they are. My mama knows and so does Violet. It was an idea I had even before ladies got the right to vote in Colorado this year.

Maybe someday I'll tell you what it is if you tell me a secret of yours in return. Have you got any, Melinda?"

Looking her in the eye, I said, "You bet I have. It has to do with Goldendale, and we've only been here a couple of days. I can't tell you about it yet, though."

"I love secrets," said Violet happily.

We found Edward Gideon at the Potter house, a place I had thought I'd never see again. He was asleep on their front porch, and Mrs. Potter was sitting in a porch swing sketching him. She looked up as the three of us came through her front gate and put her finger to her lips, motioning toward Edward Gideon.

"Poor beast," she said softly. "He must have had a bad night to sleep so heavily." Now she peered at me and exclaimed, "Well, it's little Melinda Carpenter, isn't it? I'd heard you and Sally were staying here in town for a while. What brings you back here to us, Melinda?" Oh, how sweet she was being!

I pointed to Edward Gideon. "Him! I've come to bring him home to Judge Garway's house. That's my job now." I went up onto the porch and knelt down beside the dog. I said very softly so Esther and Violet couldn't hear me, "Mrs. Potter, no one knows about what happened between your son and my sister. Have you told anybody?"

How cross she looked as she hissed softly, "No, I have not. I realize that a marriage based on pity is a bad thing.

I will not write my boy that you are still here. Rest assured on that score. Hopefully he'll find a California girl whom he really loves soon."

As I snapped the leash onto the dog's collar and shook him awake, I whispered back, "I hope he does, too." Then aloud I said, "Come on, Edward Gideon, let's go home." Danged if I wanted to come here often to catch him. But if I had to, I would!

Esther, Violet, a sleepy Edward Gideon, and I were just heading down Elm when suddenly a big, fat firecracker came sailing out over the fence of the house next door to the Potters. It lit six feet from us and exploded with a frightful *bang*. The dog started off at a gallop with me running behind him. As I raced along, I looked back over my shoulder and saw Stump howling happily, jumping up and down. He threw the firecracker! It was probably one he'd saved up from the last Fourth of July celebration. How I wished I could shake my fist at him, but I had to keep both hands on the leash and move my legs as fast as I could.

"Hang on, Melinda!" cried Esther, running on one side of me.

"Don't let go, Melinda," shouted Violet from the other side. "Dig in your heels."

I gritted my teeth, squared my shoulders, dug in my heels, and sailed along behind the big dog. Danged if I'd fall down and lose him with that hateful Stump watching me.

I yelled, *"Whoa, Edward Gideon, whoa!"* but he didn't slow down until we reached Main Street.

After all the excitement of the afternoon, I was thankful that the next day, Saturday, was quiet. I spent it dog watching in the judge's backyard. Edward Gideon didn't leave the yard all day while I was there, but while we ate supper he jumped the fence again.

The next morning the judge, Sarah Jane, and I walked to the Protestant church. It was a nice wooden building, which I was pretty certain had been ordered from a catalog like many of the other buildings in Goldendale. The services were a lot like those we went to at home, and I knew all the hymns we sang.

Violet and her family were in a pew across from the judge's pew. The Potters were also in church. When we came out, I spotted them in the rear. Sarah Jane must have, too, because she turned her head fast to look away from their direction. We left before they made it out to shake hands with the minister.

Though I had craned my neck looking for Esther and her folks, I couldn't find them. I supposed they went to the other church in town, the Catholic one.

After church Violet went dog hunting with me. As

usual, I started for the Pronghorn Hotel, but before we got there, Esther hailed us. She was standing out in front of her store and she had Edward Gideon on a rope!

I ran up to her and said, "Oh, but you are a true-blue pal, Esther. How long have you had him? Didn't catching him keep you from going to church today?"

"Melinda, I don't go to church here."

"You don't? Why not?"

"Because I'm Jewish. Jewish people don't go to churches."

"Well, where do Jewish people go then?"

"We go to a temple or a synagogue. But there aren't any in Goldendale." Esther looked very serious. "There aren't enough Jewish people here to have one. There's only us Mittelmans and Mr. Bauman, the old bachelor druggist. We have a Friday-night supper to celebrate the coming of our Sabbath, and Papa and my brothers study the Torah and Talmud with Mr. Bauman; but with only five men we haven't got enough for a *minyan*."

"A *minyan*. What's that?"

She sighed. "Nobody ever seems to know that word. A *minyan* is ten men who are Jewish. Ten men are needed for Jews to hold Sabbath services in a temple and be blessed by the presence of the Shekinah. That spirit comes whenever there are ten men together."

This was news to me. I'd never really gotten to know

any Jewish families or Jewish classmates in Chicago. I asked, "And until there are ten Jewish men here, you can't have a church, huh?"

"That's right. Even if Goldendale is a friendly town, it makes Mama sad that there aren't any other Jewish ladies here to talk to about our customs and cooking and holidays. It gets lonesome for her with just me to talk to about those things. Papa says we ought to be glad we're in a town where Jewish people aren't bothered because they are Jewish. He got cussed out for being Jewish when he was a boy back East and had rocks thrown at him once. But Mama's lonesome. The other women give church parties and suppers and go to sewing circles the church has, but not her." Esther paused, then went on. "I'm luckier than Mama is. I have Violet as a friend and now I have you, too, but Mama doesn't have anybody her own age who'd understand some of the things she wants to talk about. Besides, she doesn't work on Saturday, which is our Sabbath, or *Shabbes,* when most ladies come into the store to shop. Papa and my brothers work then because they have to, but not Mama. She is a rabbi's daughter and was brought up very strictly. A rabbi is sort of like a Jewish minister. Mama feels she ought to stay inside on the Sabbath, as she was taught."

This was sure a lot of facts to take in all at once, but as Esther was talking, I made up my mind to take a hand in the matter of a *minyan.* My brain started working on an idea. Like some of them, this one came very fast. But if it worked, Mrs. Mittelman's lonesomeness could be coming to an end very soon, and I'd be doing a good deed.

I asked Esther, "Have you ever tried to get a *minyan* here?"

"No. How could we?"

"You could get a *minyan* the way people get anything else in this country. If we can get into your store right now, I'll show you how."

"Sure we can. I have a key to the side door in my pocket."

I handed Edward Gideon's leash to Violet to hold and followed Esther into the store. I borrowed some paper and ink and thumbtacks, and in ten minutes I was done. It took another ten minutes to lock up the store again and walk to the train depot, where we put up the sign I'd lettered so people passing through on trains would spot it. It read:

THIS IS GOLDENDALE, COLORADO. IT NEEDS A MIN-YAN. IF YOU KNOW WHAT A MINYAN IS, PLEASE GET OFF HERE AND ASK MR. AARON MITTELMAN ABOUT IT AT MITTELMAN'S EMPORIUM.

I was proud of myself and the admirable job I'd done. I patted Edward Gideon, whose tongue was lolling out, and said, "There! That ought to do it. That's how Uncle Julius got the best foundryman he ever hired. He put up a sign in a place where people would see it."

Violet breathed, "I heard about *minyans* a long time back from Esther. I could have put up a sign but didn't."

Esther said, "No, Violet, it's my religion and my *minyan*. Why didn't I think about doing this?"

I told them both, "You didn't think about it because you aren't from a big city like Chicago, Illinois. This is the Chicago way of getting things done. We advertise!"

~6~
My Friends, the _Minyan_, and Me

I supposed I should have told Sarah Jane and the judge about my helping get a _minyan_. I didn't though. After all, a person shouldn't go about bragging about her good deeds. I went back quietly to Cedar Street with Edward Gideon in tow, and ate a Sunday dinner of roast chicken like I hadn't done anything at all out of the ordinary that day.

As I helped my sister wash the dishes afterwards, I asked, "Sarah Jane, did you talk with Mr. and Mrs. Potter after I left church to go look for the judge's dog?"

"No, Melinda, I only caught a glimpse of them driving off in their wagon. I don't think they want to deal with me either. I wonder how _he_ explained my breaking off the engagement to his parents. I shudder to think. He must have as queer an opinion of me as I have of him. The

Potter wagon was already following a black one that had been waiting outside the church when I came out. The judge and I walked past it, and the two men inside lifted their hats to me, which I must say is a thing some men fail to do here in Colorado."

A black wagon with two men inside? And the Potters following it? I asked, "Did the two men in the black wagon have yellow hair and yellow mustaches? And did one have a piece of glass in his eye?"

"That's right. One of them had a monocle."

I nodded. They were the English honourables, all right. And they needed Mr. Potter for some reason, even on Sunday. I wished I could have a gander at their castle on the plains. Well, maybe I could at that. After all, one of them had called Sarah Jane a handsome gel. If he became interested in her, he would surely ask her to see his castle, and maybe I could go along, too. But first I'd have to get him to ask her.

I said, "Sarah Jane, do you suppose you could wear that lilac-colored silk dress from your trousseau to church next week? You wore that brown traveling costume today. You look a lot prettier in lilac than in brown, even if you did wear a bird-of-paradise hat."

Suddenly she slammed down a skillet into the sink and said, "Melinda, that silk dress was to be my second-best gown after my wedding dress!"

Such a fuss! I said, "Well, why not get some use out

of it? You can't sashay around anywhere in the wedding gown and veil, but you could doll up in the lilac one. There are other fish in the sea besides him."

Sarah Jane scowled at me as she said, "I know about the fish in the sea. An attorney friend of the judge's met me after church and asked me to accompany him to a ball at the Oddfellows Lodge next Saturday night."

"Are you going?"

"No. I thanked him and politely refused."

"Was he a masher?"

"No, he was a perfectly proper young man. I could tell the judge liked him, but I don't want to go out in society for a while. I am content with the way things are, Melinda. When I am ready, I shall go out."

"What excuse did you give the young man?"

"I told him a lie. I got the idea for it from you. I said that I had recently had sad news about a friend who had drowned in San Francisco Bay and I simply did not feel up to dancing. He said he understood."

This made me sad, but at least Sarah Jane had got noticed here, and fast, too. I hoped she'd get over her sorrow quickly. It would be just dandy if an honourable asked her to ride out with him to see the castle. She'd surely want me along as a chaperone. I was sure that the intentions of any honourable would be honorable, too. After all, they were English gentlemen. If I had to, I would take a hand in getting her invited by one of them.

But right now I'd give the situation some time.

After wiping the last cup, I started out with a plate of leftovers for Edward Gideon, in case he hadn't already left. As I walked past the study, the judge, who had been reading the newspaper, called me in. He asked, "How do you like it here in Goldendale?"

"Tolerably well, I guess."

"Are you getting to know the town?"

"Yes, sir, at least the parts of it where Edward Gideon visits, like the hotel, stores, saloons, and some homes." I added, "He goes to houses like Mrs. Potter's."

"Well, well," said Judge Garway, as he put his paper down. "Does the dog go there, too? That's news to me. So Mrs. Potter feeds him?"

"She used to give him special meat cookies."

He laughed and said, "The Potters are rather interesting people."

I said, "Mrs. Potter is artistic. Is Mr. Potter?"

"No. I've known them for years. He's a businessman. Currently he's a sort of contractor-purchasing agent for two young English noblemen who are importing a castle and erecting it on the plains. I have not met them, but I am told they are rather eccentric."

"Eccentric?"

"Odd. Different. But then as titled Britishers they would be different here. They and the menservants they brought over with them keep to themselves." Now the judge saw the tin pie plate in my hands and said, "You're taking that out to my dog?"

"Yes, sir, I am."

"Well, I hope you find him, but I doubt it. Sometimes he waits until my dinner is over, then takes off. Other times he doesn't wait. It isn't as if he doesn't get handouts elsewhere."

"Judge, have you ever asked people not to feed him? Maybe if you do that, he'll have to come home to eat."

"I have done that very thing. I took out a notice in the newspaper asking people not to give him food. It did not a whit of good. They feed him all the same. I have been told that no one can resist the expression in his eyes."

I didn't say anything. I suspected it was more his size than his eyes. He was a nice dog, but just his size would be enough to give plenty of folks the willies if they figured he was hungry. Edward Gideon was an awful lot of dog! When he sat down, he could rest his chin on the tablecloth and watch every mouthful we ate with sad, begging eyes.

The judge seemed to be in a chatty mood, so I thought I'd ask him about something that was on my mind. I said, "I've made some friends here already, and they told me about how you would like to have your own courthouse because you're cramped where you are now. They say you're going to hold court in a saloon any day now."

"Well, for a newcomer here you're surely well up on things, aren't you? Who told you all this?"

"Esther Mittelman and Violet Stowe."

"Ah, that pair. They're a sturdy twosome. You're in good hands with them, Melinda."

I said, "Thank you. I like them a lot. With me they're in good hands, too. Sir, don't you think a saloon court would annoy the ladies? It seems to me they could have helped you get a courthouse. Would you really hold a court in a saloon?"

"I'm not sure. But I have noticed when I threaten that, it makes the voters sit up and take notice. Now, go feed my animal if you can find him. I want to get on with my paper."

On Monday we got a letter from Aunt Rhoda. It arrived so soon after we wrote her that she must have written it the very minute she got ours. It was mostly from her. Aunt Rhoda wrote that she was "very mortified" for Sarah Jane that Edgar Everett would think she was lonely. She felt sorry for his parents but "rejoiced" in my sister's courage in not going on to California and marrying such a "ridiculous" person. She approved of the telegram I'd sent him but didn't seem fazed by the one I wrote them. Aunt Rhoda said she'd even used my idea and told Sarah Jane's friends that this is what had happened, and that Sarah Jane was grieving with her late betrothed's parents in their Colorado home. She added that everyone appreciated my sister's noble gesture.

Uncle Julius added a P.S. for me. It said:

Melinda, don't send any more of your interesting telegrams. Write letters instead, they're cheaper. Look out for your big sister and yourself. Don't take any wooden nickels. Send us a photograph of that big dog you're watching, if you can get him to stand still long enough.

That was all from Chicago. I'd write again soon and tell them everything was dandy here. It would only upset them to know how red and puffy Sarah Jane's eyes were in the mornings and how she sometimes wiped them on her apron when she thought nobody was watching.

All during the next week, Esther, Violet, and I had the *minyan* on our minds. Nobody had got off any train to ask about it at Mittelman's store. But the sign was still up. Esther said she'd gone to see it three times. Wanting to keep it a nice surprise, she hadn't told anybody in her family about my making it; because hired draymen fetched goods off the trains to their store, none of the busy Mittelman men saw it.

Finally, after it had been up on the depot wall for eight

days, we got news about it. Esther, Violet, a just-caught
Edward Gideon, and I were outside the Mittelman Emporium. Mr. Potter and the two English honourables had
just gone inside when we saw the stationmaster come
stumping along the boardwalk toward us. He looked at
the three of us and at the dog, nodded, then went inside.
A moment later we heard Mr. Mittelman's voice shouting
out, "What? What's that you say? What sign? Where?
Where is it? On the depot wall?"

Esther let out a wail. "Papa's mad."

We listened to the drone of the stationmaster's deep
voice though we were too far away to hear what he said.

Nobody could miss what Mr. Mittelman said, though.
He was yelling now. "A sign on the depot wall asking
for men to come to my store to make up a *minyan*? No,
sir! I didn't tack it up. Why should I pay you for the space
it takes up? Is this somebody's idea of a joke? Nobody
advertises for a sacred thing. Come here you, Joshua, Sam,
Ben—I want to talk to you boys!"

I looked at Esther, who had gone very pale. She looked
at me and asked, "Oh, Melinda, what'll we do now?"

Violet offered, "Run like the dickens." Then she said,
"No, pretend we don't know anything about it at all."

I asked, "Esther, will you get a licking because of this?"

"No, but I'll sure get yelled at."

"No, you won't. I did it, not you." I took a deep breath

to the bottom of my lungs, got a strong hold on Edward Gideon's collar, and went inside the store, where the five men were bellowing at each other. Mrs. Mittelman was standing behind the yard-goods counter, holding a bolt of pink checkered gingham in front of her as if it was going to protect her.

I looked behind me and saw that Violet and Esther had followed me. They were brave girls. Raising my voice, I shouted over the men's deep voices, *"I did it! Me, Melinda. I made that sign."*

Because my voice was high-pitched, they heard me. Everybody in the store turned around to stare. Edward Gideon knew something was wrong. He barked one of his deep barks, then began to rumble a growl in his chest.

Mr. Mittelman, whose beard seemed to be standing out on all sides because of his anger, shouted at me, "You, you girl! Did you say you put up a sign about a *minyan* in the depot?"

"Yes, sir. I did."

"Why? Why did you do that? You aren't even Jewish!"

"No, sir, I'm not, but your daughter's my pal. She told me how important a *minyan* was, and I wanted to do something nice for her because she's been a good friend to me."

Mrs. Mittelman flung down the bolt of gingham and cried out, *"Aaron!"*

"Mama," shouted Esther, who fled behind the cloth counter to be held tightly by her mother.

"Aaron," repeated Mrs. Mittelman sharply, "the girls meant no harm. They were only trying to do a good thing. I know Melinda."

It seemed to me that Mr. Mittelman's beard was drawing in. He gave me a long, hard look, then said to the stationmaster, "I'm sorry I got so riled up just now, Gus. Please take the sign down. I'll be glad to pay you for the days it was up. Sorry I yelled at you."

"It don't matter, Aaron. Are you sure you want it hauled down?"

Mr. Mittelman sighed. "Yes, take it down. That's not the right way to get a *minyan.*"

A store customer asked, "Say, Aaron, what's a *minyan* anyhow?"

After Mr. Mittelman explained what it was, I heard one of the honourables saying in a high-pitched voice, "Why, I think posting a poster was a deuced clever idea on the part of a mere child."

Mr. Potter, who stood fairly close to me, muttered, "I strongly suspect that that girl there with the dog is no mere child, Mr. Farnsworth-Jones."

The people around Mr. Potter chuckled at his comment. I wasn't sure whether he meant it as a compliment or not, but didn't ask.

The stationmaster nodded and went out. After he left,

Mrs. Mittelman walked up to me and said, "Melinda, we know you meant well, but you don't know our religion. What you did was not dignified."

"Mama, Mama," prompted Esther, pulling at her mother's sleeve.

Mrs. Mittelman smiled and said, "Esther's been wanting me to ask you and Violet to a family Sabbath supper. I was going to ask you to next Friday's, but I think now I'd better let Aaron simmer down a bit first."

I said, "Oh, sure, I understand. Can Esther walk the judge's dog home with me now though?"

Mrs. Mittelman gave her daughter a small push and said, "Yes, it would be better if she was away from here for a little while."

Once we were outside, Esther said, "Papa likes you, Melinda."

"What makes you think so?"

Esther smiled. "I can tell. He didn't call you any names in Yiddish. Yiddish is the other language we speak. It's a sort of German and Hebrew mixed up together and is just full of special names for people who get your goat."

As the three of us started for the judge's house with Edward Gideon, Esther went on, "I wish Papa and Mama didn't have to find out about the sign in front of so many people. It was embarrassing for everybody."

I said, "You bet it was. For me, too."

As we came abreast of the town's only drug store,

which was also its only ice cream parlor, I told my friends, "Judge Garway paid me for my dog catching Saturday night, so I'm rich. I want to buy some ice cream sodas for all of us."

Violet said, "I wouldn't say no to chocolate. Esther likes strawberry best."

I said, "I love maple, but I'll settle for anything that's ice cream. I wonder what Edward Gideon likes."

Esther said, "He isn't particular. He'll eat any kind anyone gives him. It gets his nose cold, but he doesn't stop eating."

"Could I take him inside?"

Violet answered me, "I think so, as long as he's on a leash."

A couple of minutes later we were seated at a white metal table sipping sodas. Edward Gideon had already gulped down a vanilla-flavored ice cream cone and only sneezed once when he got ice cream up his nose. After that, he lay down beside my chair, licking his chops and looking contented.

As Esther drew the last of her soda up through her straw, she said, "Melinda, I think it's time for me to tell you my secret. I owe it to you for taking all the blame for the sign. Will you tell me your secret if I tell you mine?"

I looked from Esther to Violet, then I nodded and said, "Okay, but you go first, though."

"Promise me you won't laugh."

"I won't laugh."

Esther leaned toward me and said, "I want to be a real pioneer in my life. I want to be a lady rabbi when I grow up."

I was amazed. "You mean a sort of woman minister?"

"That's right. Papa and my brothers don't know what I want to be, but Mama says it would be wonderful. She got a letter from some lady friends out in California who tell her that a Jewish lady out there has already studied to become a rabbi. Her name's Rachel Frank."

I asked, "Esther, will it be hard to become one?"

"Oh, yes, it is for every man, too. I'll have to go to special schools. It would take me years and years to learn all a rabbi has to know. And lots of folks in my religion won't like the idea of a girl becoming one, but I plan to try."

"But, Esther, I've never heard of a lady minister. Uncle Julius would have a fit if I told him that's what I wanted to be."

"Yes, I know that's true among Christians, too. I'll have to leave Goldendale to go to a special college, but when the time comes, I'm going. I'm already studying the Hebrew language with my brothers." She jerked her head toward the druggist and whispered, "Mr. Bauman teaches us on Thursday nights. He doesn't know either what I want to be. Well, Melinda, I've told you my secret. Now what's yours?"

"Esther, it isn't really my secret. It belongs to my sister, Sarah Jane, and to the Potter family."

Violet asked, "Mr. and Mrs. Potter?"

I nodded, then told my pals all about the prune sculpture at the Exposition, Edgar Everett Potter and my sister, the telegrams, and how we got to be stranded in Goldendale. As I finished with the words, "And I can hear her crying at night in her room," both friends lifted wet eyes to look at me.

Esther said, "What a wicked thing for him to do. If he'd thought she was lonesome, he should have told her that in Chicago."

Violet added, "Yes, she could have hit him over the head with that box of prunes he gave her. Those were dandy telegrams you sent, Melinda."

I nodded. "I know I shouldn't brag, but I sort of liked them, too." Then I sighed. "But Sarah Jane doesn't seem to want to sashay out with any men here. She's already refused an invitation to go to a ball."

Violet said, "She's awful pretty, but she does look sad."

"She is. She hasn't got over him yet. That's why."

Violet exploded. "Melinda, you ought to write that galoot and tell him what for. Give it to him hammer and tongs for insulting your sister!"

Should I? That idea hadn't occurred to me.

While I was thinking about this, Esther said, "No, Melinda, you shouldn't write him. He doesn't deserve a letter. He's a dirty hound. Don't waste paper and ink and your hand muscles. You don't want him to answer you and have your sister find out you wrote him, do you?"

"You are right, Esther Mittelman. Much as I'd enjoy writing him, I will take your advice."

With these words, I got up, gave Edward Gideon's leash a little tug to get him going, and paid Mr. Bauman my fifteen cents. Just as we got to the door, though, it opened and in came portly, white-whiskered Dr. Harmon, one of the town's three doctors. He lifted his black-silk top hat to the three of us, smiled at Edward Gideon, then said, laughing, "I was just down at your folks' emporium, Esther, buying some new harness for my buggy. I heard about the sign you kids put up. That news is all over town."

Esther asked, "Did you see my papa? Is he laughing about it?"

"Yes, he sold me the harness, but he wasn't laughing, though. He seemed pretty matter-of-fact about it and told me that you three took a lot on yourselves doing it."

By now Mr. Bauman had come out of the little room where he'd been pounding his medicines. He asked, "What's this about a sign?"

The doctor jerked a thumb at Esther and said, "Ask

Esther here, Jacob. She had a part in it, I hear."

I kept quiet as Esther told Mr. Bauman what I'd put on the sign. For a moment he looked surprised, then he chuckled and said, "Well, it wasn't dignified, but nobody could say it wasn't enterprising." He shook his head. "Yes, it would be fine to have a *minyan* here. Nobody can deny that. But if a *minyan* comes here to Goldendale, it'll have to come naturally. We can't very well snag men off the trains passing through. I imagine it's going to take some time before we have one since we aren't likely to get another big family of sons like the Mittelmans all in one fell swoop. Families aren't as inclined to come West as single Jewish men are."

Dr. Harmon was looking at Esther as he said, "This is all most interesting. I learned something this afternoon that I didn't know. I'd always thought a preacher and one listener made up a church the way a teacher at one end of a log and a pupil at the other make up a school. It seems to be more formal with Jews, doesn't it?"

Mr. Bauman agreed.

"Yes. Well, Jake, I need you to make up a batch of tonic for me now. Good day to you, girls." The doctor tipped his hat again and went into the little room with the druggist. We also left.

Out on the boardwalk, Esther told me, "I think you better talk with your sister, Melinda, about seeing other gents. Some of them could be interesting. There are two bachelor doctors and a lot of lawyers, farmers, and miners. But if she got tied up with a miner, she'd have to go up into the hills and get snowed in all winter."

I asked, "How about the two English galoots, Esther? How well do you know them?"

"I've talked to them in the store once, that's all. My papa knows them better. They are very polite to Mama. She thinks they may be related by blood to Queen Victoria."

Related to the queen of England! I felt dizzy and my head reeled. Royal blood? Royal blood came to Goldendale!

7

The Red Bandanna

Because it wasn't my way to let grass grow under my feet, I planned to have a talk with Sarah Jane the minute I got home with Edward Gideon. I couldn't, though, because she was in the parlor playing a shiny brown spinet piano that hadn't been there that morning.

Holding onto the dog, I asked in surprise, "Where'd that piano come from?"

Still playing the Strauss waltz she used to play in Chicago, she said, "Off the Denver train this morning. Judge Garway ordered it last week as soon as he found out that I could play." As she put the cover down over the keyboard, she went on, "Melinda, I don't tell you everything that goes on, you know."

I flared up. "You used to! You'd tell me just about everything that happened to you!"

"We aren't in Chicago anymore. Times have changed and I have changed with them."

"Well, not me. I haven't changed!"

"I can see that very well, indeed. Please release that animal in the backyard before he wags his tail in here again and knocks over another vase the way he did last week."

I told Edward Gideon, "Come on, dog, we aren't welcome in here." And out we went. I sat on the back steps dog watching and thinking things over until Sarah Jane called me inside to peel potatoes and scrub carrots before she put them on to cook.

After supper she played the piano for the judge, who nodded his head in time to her music. I listened, too, and noticed that she played melancholy music, mostly Stephen Foster's sad tunes. She played "Oh, Susanna" when the judge asked for it, but she surely dragged it out.

When he asked if she knew "The Camptown Races," she told him, "No, I haven't got any sheet music with me. I'm playing by memory, and I never did know that tune."

I almost gasped out loud. That was a lie. It was Uncle Julius's favorite song, and I'd heard her play it lots of times. She just didn't want to play it because it was lively.

When she came up to bed at ten o'clock, I went next door to her room and tapped on her door. "It's me, Melinda. I got to talk with you."

Her voice was low. "Won't tomorrow do?"

"No, it won't. Now is the hour."

"All right. Come in."

So I went in and found her brushing her long hair before she got into her nightclothes. In a minute she'd braid it for bed to keep it from snarling.

"What is it, Melinda?"

As I sat down on her bed, I said, "It's you, Sarah Jane. I'm worried about you."

She went on brushing. "Well, don't you be. I'm quite content here. It's peaceful. I like the quiet and the fresh air and the view of the western mountains. I wrote Aunt Rhoda this morning that we are staying on and asked her to send out our heavy winter clothing. I've heard that it snows quite a bit here. You'll remember that I'd thought of going to New York, but Judge Garway told me that times are hard there and it might be difficult for me to obtain work. So why go? I trust his judgment. After all, he is a judge. I've scouted Goldendale a bit and learned that a business school is to start up here very soon. It will offer courses in typewriting and bookkeeping on Thursdays, my day off. I plan to enroll. When we leave Goldendale, I will be qualified for things other than housework, but until that time comes, I shall stay on here." She turned to look at me and said, "Melinda, you could go back to Chicago now if you want to."

I shook my head. "No! I'll stay, too. I've started school and I've made some friends." I played my ace now. "Besides, I tore up the yellow card Aunt Rhoda had made for me to wear on my train ride home."

Sarah Jane smiled slightly, then sighed. "Yes, I had noticed that it was missing when I unpacked. I didn't think it important enough to take up with you."

"I didn't ever need it anyhow. Sarah Jane, please don't make me go home without you!"

She sighed again and began to braid her hair, her fingers moving fast. "All right, Melinda. Thank you for wanting to stay with me."

"You're my only sister, aren't you?"

"And you're mine!" She gave me another smile that encouraged me.

"Sarah Jane, you're pretty. Everybody tells me how pretty you are. I think you ought to let the Goldendale gents squire you around. *He* isn't the only fish in the duck pond. Step out with the judge if he asks you to. Didn't he get the piano for you?"

"No, Melinda. Though the judge is not so old as he appears, he wants to remain a lifelong bachelor. As for the piano, he got it for the music, not really for me. His older sister had wanted to learn how to play it, but she never found the time. He said he had intended to get a piano someday in any event. My being here to play it only speeded up his ordering it. The judge says he might take piano lessons himself someday."

Sarah sounded so final about the judge that I decided

to change the subject. I said, "I got in trouble today with the Mittelmans."

She stopped braiding and asked me, "What did you do?"

"I tried to be helpful to them." Now I told her about the *minyan* and the sign I'd made and how mad Mr. Mittelman had been because of it. I also mentioned what Mr. Potter said about me in Mittelman's Emporium.

Sarah Jane shook her head and said, "Oh, Melinda, you should not have done that. A *minyan* is a holy thing to Jewish people. You be careful from now on! And as for Mr. Potter and his remarks, I'd be very grateful if you would not talk to me about any of the Potter family again. I am quite sure that *he* is already courting some girl out in California, now that I have married a railroad conductor."

"Well, if you think that, why don't you let somebody court you? Just because you go out, you don't have to get yourself engaged again, now that you know how dangerous it can be."

She stood up, frowned, then said, "Yes, I think you are probably right. I should not bury myself here in housework, the piano, the judge's books, business courses, and church once a week. I should be more sociable, I suppose."

This got me up off her bed. "That's the ticket! You ought to see some of the pretty country around here before it snows. See the mountains and the rivers and the prairie and other towns in this state—maybe even Denver."

"Yes, I should see them and get photographs of the scenery to send home to Chicago. I'd planned to send pictures from California, but Colorado will have to do. You should see the countryside, too, Melinda."

"I want to. I surely want to see everything I can see."

I decided not to tell her that what I most wanted to see was the honourables' castle, not to mention the honourables themselves. If she thought I wanted her to get acquainted with folks who might be blood relatives of Queen Victoria, she might balk.

After I kissed her and said good-night, I went out into the hallway and stood there for a long time thinking. The Sarah Jane I had known in Chicago was not the same one I just finished talking with in Goldendale. She was deeper than she used to be, thanks to Edgar Everett Potter III. Because she didn't seem inclined to flirt now, it would be up to me to take a hand in getting the honourables and Sarah Jane together. I wasn't fussy about which one took an interest in her. I was glad there were two of them, because it doubled my chances that one of the honourables would take to her.

On the way back to my room, I looked out the rear hallway window to see if I could spot Edward Gideon.

Although there wasn't much light, I was able to see that there wasn't any big, black dog in the backyard. He'd flown the coop again.

Back inside my room, I went over to my own window to look out onto Cedar Street and see if I could spot the judge's dog anywhere. I could hear whistling. As I listened to the trills and bird sounds, I remembered who whistled that way. *Stump!* The sounds he made at school were so loud they hurt everybody's ears. Miss Hawkins had to yell "Stop it" at him whenever he did it. Yes, there he was, riding around in circles in the middle of Cedar Street with his arms folded, not touching the handlebars. I wished Edward Gideon were here to chase him away, but I was sure the doggoned dog was at the Bonanza Palace Saloon, where, I was told, he always stayed until eleven o'clock.

Sticking my fingers into my ears to shut out the whistling noises, I got into bed and pulled the bedclothes over my head. Stump meant to let me know he was out there. His being outside wasn't any accident. I knew that he wanted me to kick up a fuss at school tomorrow about his pestering me now. Well, I was too smart for him. I'd fix his wagon by not letting on at all that I'd heard or seen him. I had more important things on my mind—the honourables and Sarah Jane.

*   *   *

The first thing I did before school was to ask Esther how her papa had behaved to her yesterday evening, whether he had gotten mad at us all over again.

She told me, "No, we talked about the sign at supper. He was a little out of sorts about it, but Mama had fixed chicken his favorite way, so he calmed down while he ate."

Violet said, "My ma does that, too, when Pa's riled up about something one of us has done. It works just fine on him. With him it's pork chops and gravy. When he's eating, he can't be yelling, too."

I nodded. Aunt Rhoda made roast beef and cabbage when Uncle Julius got his dander up. When I opened the front door of our house and smelled cabbage fumes, I stepped lightly and politely, believe me.

I now changed the subject and told my two friends about my talk with Sarah Jane last night and her decision to start going out. I said, "I think she's willing to be courted—not eager, but willing."

Violet clapped her hands. "Oh, that's fine, Melinda."

"I need you both to help me think up ways to get her courted by those English honourables."

"Both of them?" asked Violet.

"No, one at a time. It could lead to trouble the other way. I don't want anybody fighting duels over my sister. She—"

Just then the two big, brown-haired prairie boys who sat in the last row at school came abreast of us. The biggest one, whose nickname was Gar, looked Esther, Violet, and me over with cold, pale-blue eyes. Turning to Esther, he scowled at her and said in a rough, low voice, "Pa and Will and me heard tell from the stationmaster this morning that you put up a sign on the depot wall to fetch more folks like you here to Goldendale, Essie Mittelman."

Because that wasn't how it happened, I told Gar, "She didn't do that, I did! I made the sign and tacked it up."

He grinned at me and said, "So it was you, the skinny, smart-aleck new gal from Chicago who's been to see the fair when nobody else here ever has. Well, this ain't your town. You remember that. Now that I know what that sign means, I don't want to see another one like it anywheres in Goldendale."

I flared at him. "You won't see another one, but you wouldn't understand why it was taken down even if I told you, Gar."

Gar didn't say anything else. He just turned away and went into the schoolhouse, trailed by his slightly smaller brother, leaving me with my hands on my hips glaring after him.

After the two of them were gone, Esther said, "Melinda, I'm sorry you had to listen to that. Gar and his folks have never liked us Mittelmans. The sign made them mad. Papa told me and my brothers to expect to hear things like that. He heard it lots of times when he was a kid back East, and he hated it. We don't hear it so often out here in the West, but sometimes we still do. Gar and his family don't like Jewish people. His folks don't trade at our store. They drive to Heberville, though that's a good distance out of their way." She let out a little sigh and shrugged her shoulders.

I thought she was being too nice about it and was ransacking my mind for something cussing to say about Gar and his family, but before I could Miss Hawkins herded us inside. To get Esther's mind off Gar's cruel remarks, I whispered to my friends, "Forget about Gar. Think about the honourables and how I can get them together with Sarah Jane. Let me know what you come up with at recess."

During that morning's lessons I stopped thinking about Gar, too. In fact, my mind was more on Sarah Jane than on decimals and how to figure compound interest, things I usually did well. From the sorry work Violet and Esther did at the blackboard, I was pretty sure that their minds weren't on mathematics anymore than mine was.

We got together at recess under the big cottonwood tree by the little creek at the edge of the school ground. Violet's idea was for Sarah Jane and me to rent a rig, learn the direction of the castle, and drive out and call on the honourables.

I said, "No, we can't do that. It's not like calling on new next-door neighbors. We're newer here than they are. Besides, neither of us would know how to drive a rig. Sarah Jane can't even ride a horse, and I've only had two riding lessons. All right, Esther, what have you come up with?"

"Get the judge to invite them to supper at his house. That way they'll find out Sarah Jane can cook."

I thought about this for a while, then said, "It's a better idea than Violet's, but I don't think the judge would take to it. He's smart when it comes to figuring out what folks might be up to. He'd realize that I asked him to invite the honourables so I could show off my sister and maybe get her married to one of them. He'd know he'd lose a housekeeper and a dogcatcher, too." I sighed. "Besides, Sarah Jane would guess what I was up to. No, Esther, that won't work."

Esther nodded. "I guess you're right, Melinda. And as foreigners they aren't even voters. He'd be wise to that scheme."

"Okay, if no one has any other ideas, I guess I'll have to fall back on my own plan."

"What is it?" asked Violet.

As we huddled together under the tree, I told them my plan, that I intended to meet the honourables by having one of them rescue me next Saturday morning if either of them came to town. How wide their eyes got!

Esther gasped. "You might get killed. Do you know how to do that, Melinda?"

"Not really, but I've read about it plenty of times in books. Lady characters are always doing it."

Violet wanted to know, "But is it done in England so the honourables would know what they're supposed to do?"

"Oh, sure, it's done in droves over there, so any Englishman ought to know all about it by now. I'm going to need help from both of you, though."

"What do you want us to do?" asked Esther.

"One of you will keep watch for an honourable coming in to Goldendale. The other one will have to corral Edward Gideon and hang onto him so he doesn't get in my way or get hurt."

Violet asked, "Can we watch you, Melinda?"

"No, you won't be close enough to see me. But I'll tell you all about it later. I'm not going to enjoy doing this, but it ought to work. Anyway, I've just got to try! I want to hear my sister laugh again. She hasn't laughed once since she got that letter from Edgar Everett Potter III."

With everything arranged beforehand with Esther and Violet, I took up my planned station in one of the chairs outside the Pronghorn Hotel early Saturday morning. I'd already collared Edward Gideon moseying along Main Street and had taken him to Violet's house. Esther had come out of her family's store at eight forty-five, waved at me, and gone away up the street toward the dirt road that led into Goldendale from the prairie. I had Judge Garway's sister's silver-plated mother-of-pearl opera glasses with me. All I had to do was sit tight and keep looking through them until I saw Esther flap a big red bandanna at me. A red one would let me know that the honourables were approaching and that I should spring into action. If she waved a blue one, it meant that Mr. Potter was with them. In that case, I'd go to Violet's house, get Edward Gideon, and wait for the next Saturday.

I sat and sat and sat. Folks walking past on the boardwalk stared at me looking through my opera glasses. I stared back at them. I saw Stump Wood at a distance and stuck out my tongue at him even though I knew he couldn't see me at all.

Finally I saw it—a scarlet flapping halfway down Main Street. I set the opera glasses down carefully beside my chair and came to the edge of the boardwalk. I inspected the street in front of me. There were some puddles in it from last night's shower. I sighed. I'd hoped for a drier street, but who knew if I'd have the chance next Saturday. I'd better do it now.

I watched as a red-wheeled black wagon with a black-fringed canopy pulled by a team of grays trotting smartly in front came towards me. Yes, it was the honourable's spring wagon, and Mr. Alfred was driving alone.

When the fancy two-seater was some twenty feet from me, I stepped into the street, walking as if I were crossing to the other side of Main. I took seven steps, flung up my arms shouting out *"Alas!"* and sank slowly to my knees, then flat onto the ground. Unfortunately, one arm fell into a mud puddle. I had "swooned," just like I'd been practicing secretly for days.

"Whoa, whoa, halt there! I say, halt!" a man's high-pitched voice yelled.

I opened one eye and saw that the honourables' horses had stopped so close to me that one of them was slobbering on my skirt. I felt like shuddering, but didn't dare. Folks who fainted didn't move a muscle.

Mr. Alfred got down from his seat and came running up to me. Hurrah, he knew what to do about swoons! He was bending over to pick me up, but before he got hold of me, Dr. Harmon came lumbering up, brushed him to one side, swooped me up into his arms, and shouted, "Stand back. Stand back. She's fainted. I'll take the girl into the hotel."

Hotel? I didn't want to go there. I opened my eyes and repeated what all the swooning ladies in books said, "Where am I?"

A man I'd never seen before answered me. "Golden-dale, Colorado. You passed out, little girl."

I looked from the stranger to Dr. Harmon, then to Mr.

Alfred, and said weakly to the honourable, "Take me home, please. I'll be all right. I just want to go home. I live on Cedar Street in Judge Garway's house with my sister, Sarah Jane Carpenter."

Though it was hard to do since the doctor was still holding me, I held out my arms to the honourable and cried, "Mister, please take me home to my sister before I swoon some more."

"Okay, take the child home," said the doctor, handing me like a sack of oats to Mr. Farnsworth-Jones, who smelled of lemons and leather. The honourable set me on my feet, then helped me up into his wagon where I sat looking as limp as possible.

8

I Am Entertained!

Sarah Jane came to the door to meet me and the honourable, who had his arm under my right elbow. I tried to look pale and shaken as she opened the door and cried, "What's wrong? What's happened to you, Melinda?"

Before Mr. Alfred could tell her, I said, "I swooned in the street."

Her mouth opened in wonder, then closed as the Honourable Mr. Alfred Farnsworth-Jones whipped off his hat and said, "I suggest we take this child into your drawing room where she may recline full length on a settee." I knew what he was saying because of all the swooning books I'd read. He meant that I should lie down in our parlor. I steered him to the room and flopped down onto the sofa. Then I begged my sister, "Sarah Jane, don't leave me! I may swoon again."

The Englishman told her, "Perhaps some vinegar on a cloth for her forehead would prove beneficial."

Vinegar? I hated the smell. All the book swooners used eau-de-cologne. I told him, "No, it wouldn't. Just leave me where I am, but don't leave me. What I need is a cup of tea."

My sister was looking down at me and frowning. Frown or no frown, she was pretty as could be in a dark-blue calico dress she'd just made. It made her eyes so dark they looked violet. She said, "Melinda, you don't ever drink tea."

"I feel like it now though."

The honourable put in, "There's nothing in the world like a cup of tea to pluck one up." He sure knew his onions.

I said, "Sarah Jane, why not make a pot for all of us."

I saw her glance at the honourable, nod, and leave for the kitchen. Good, the coast was clear for me.

I said, "Please sit down. The red chair is very comfortable. It's Judge Garway's favorite, but he isn't home now. He won't mind if you use it so long as you don't spill anything on its upholstery."

The honourable nodded and said, "I had heard you and your sister were living here."

Ha! It was good to hear that he'd not only taken notice of Sarah Jane but knew where we lived. I told him, "We've been here awhile, but all we've seen so far of

Colorado is Goldendale and what we rode through on our train ride from Chicago. Sarah Jane and I haven't seen the mountains or much of the prairie."

"That's a pity. Although it's rather wild hereabouts, there is a good deal to view."

I waited for him to invite us to view it with him in his handsome wagon, but he didn't. Instead he told me that I'd better rest now and picked up the judge's newspaper.

After he'd read for a time, I said, "I read the papers, too, but didn't this morning. Sometimes I read about Queen Victoria. I'm very interested in her. So is my sister. Is there anything in the paper about her?"

"Not that I can see."

"Do you know the queen?"

"I have been presented to her at Buckingham Palace."

This made me sit up and ask, "What did you say to her?"

"Nothing. I bowed and she smiled and gave me her hand. Then I bowed again and backed away from her presence."

"That doesn't sound like it took too long."

"It didn't."

I fell back onto the sofa and looked at the ceiling. Mr. Alfred continued reading the newspaper until Sarah Jane came in with the tea tray. Since I didn't really like tea, I filled my cup to the brim with sugar and milk to cover the taste. I sat up and sipped while Sarah Jane and the honourable talked about the autumn weather and Goldendale. My sister wasn't being exactly flirty with him, but I did see that at least she seemed a bit less drooping.

Finally he said to her, "I realize I may offend your sensibilities by asking you, but in the American West things do not go by our English rules of behavior. So I shall dare to ask you if you would care to take a drive with me out to my brother's and my ranch tomorrow afternoon? Last year my brother Bertie and I bought some prairie land ten miles from here and are doing some building on it. We are quite proud of it, and I think it interesting."

Here it was! He had asked her. I said quickly, "Oh, we sure would like that, wouldn't we, Sarah Jane? Tomorrow afternoon would be just fine for both of us." I had no intention of being left behind, especially after all I'd done to get us invited.

Both of them swiveled their heads in surprise to look at me. The honourable asked me, "Are you certain that you are up to a wagon ride over rough ground so soon after your recent swoon?"

"Oh, sure, I feel all right now. It was the tea that did it. You were right. It plucks one up just like you said."

Mr. Alfred left the house soon afterward, but not before he and Sarah Jane set a time for him to fetch us tomorrow. My sister followed him to the door to say good-bye and thank him again for bringing me home.

I got up and went to the kitchen with the tea tray. Sarah Jane came in soon afterward and glared at me, shaking her head. She put her hands on her hips and exploded. "Melinda, you may have pulled the wool over his eyes, but you haven't pulled it over mine. You've never fainted in your entire life. Nobody in our family has ever fainted that I know of. Look at me. You pretended to faint so you could meet Mr. Farnsworth-Jones, bring him here to meet me, and get him to ask me to go buggy riding with him. You planned this entire thing, didn't you, you scheming girl?"

The old Sarah Jane might not have seen through me, but the new one had, and I wasn't surprised. I told her truthfully, "Yes. I did it for you—to make you go out. After all, you told me you wanted to."

She let out her breath in exasperation, then turned away to look out the kitchen window. She said, "Yes, I did say that; I'll grant you that. We'll go out riding tomorrow with Mr. Farnsworth-Jones, but don't you do or say anything to embarrass me. Don't ask rude questions. Better yet, don't get out of my eyesight or my earshot."

"I promise. I won't." I'd planned to stick close to her to see how *she* behaved.

The Honourable Mr. Alfred called for us at three

o'clock sharp. He handed Sarah Jane up into his wagon, but left me to haul myself into the rear seat. Sarah Jane looked just elegant in her green velvet suit and beaver-fur capelet. Off we went at a trot with Goldendale staring at us as we passed.

On and on we went in the honourable's wagon over the flat prairie. Nobody did much talking. We were silent, listening to the rolling sound of the wheels and the horses' snorting. Sarah Jane occasionally mentioned the wild things we spotted, like prairie dogs sitting up on top of their burrows or darting jackrabbits. Once we saw a yellowish gray animal that resembled a dog. It stared at us and turned to trot away, still watching us over its shoulder.

Mr. Alfred pointed to it with his whip and said in disgust, "That beast was a coyote, a confounded animal if ever there was one. Your badgers, bears, and even your skunks can be borne, but not that devilish animal. My brother, Angus, and Malcolm have come to abhor them."

Coyotes didn't interest me. Castles did. So did people who lived in them. I asked, "Who are Angus and Malcolm?"

"Our Scottish servants. They are old family retainers who came with us from England."

Now he turned around to pay attention to his driving and left me to look at the prairie. It wasn't a lot more interesting from his fancy wagon than it had been from

the train windows—just mile after mile of brown-yellow
ground. There were no fences or farmhouses or plowed
and planted fields. It was grassland, with brown birds
rising up out of it as the horses passed where they lay.

As we went along, I considered the Honourable Mr.
Alfred and his brother, Mr. Bertie. I decided that they
couldn't be related by blood to Queen Victoria if Mr.
Alfred had to be introduced to her and hadn't spoken one
word when he was. All the same, if they brought servants
along with them to America, they must be plenty rich.

As for the castle, I tried to imagine what it would look
like. I'd wanted to see a real live one ever since I'd read
all about them in some novels of Sir Walter Scott that
Aunt Rhoda got me for my last birthday. I knew from
the stories that castles always had moats around them.
Moats were ditches filled with water, and I wondered
whether the honourables dug one to go with their castle.
I'd find out soon.

Finally, our wagon went down a dip and up over a
tallish rise, and I saw it just beneath us. The castle! I drew
in my breath. There was no mistaking what it was. It was
a castle for sure, big and gray and stony. All the towers
were there pushing up into the deep-blue autumn sky.
There was a drawbridge, but no moat. Except for that,
it looked just like I'd imagined it would from Sir Walter
Scott's books. There were some wood and sod buildings

to one side, which I figured belonged to the original ranch house.

Sarah Jane spoke up first in a tiny little voice. "I can't believe what my eyes are seeing! It *is* a castle, a real castle, way out here in the wilds."

Mr. Alfred told her, "Yes, I suppose the sight of it is rather startling to you Americans. It hasn't been inhabited for at least one hundred and fifty years. This castle was built by one of the first titled Farnsworths a full six hundred years ago. Father shipped it to Bertie and me as a present. It has seventy rooms. Actually, we would rather have had the family manor house of a later, more civilized period, but our younger sister uses it for a residence when she is not in London, so we got the old castle, which nobody was using."

Recalling Sir Walter's books, I asked, "Is it haunted? Have you got a ghost?"

"Oh, yes. There is said to be one of a maiden who wears a long, white gown. She was supposedly deserted by her lover, a false knight. She wanders wailing."

I asked, "Weeping and wailing?"

He shook his head. "No, just wailing, not weeping. It's said in one hand she bears a dagger that drips blood."

"Does her story say if she caught up with that no-good knight or if she killed herself with the dagger?" I pondered for a moment, then added, "But if she killed herself,

there ought to be some blood on that pure white gown.
I bet she got the galoot!"

"Melinda!" Sarah Jane turned around and gave me a
withering look. I was sure she was thinking about a
knight, too, one that was made out of California prunes.

Mr. Alfred didn't seem to notice my sister's reaction,
because he went on talking about the ghost. "I haven't
seen it, though. After all, we have not moved into the
castle yet. It's still not furnished. We live in the wooden
house behind the castle now."

By now we had pulled up to the castle's big, wide-open
drawbridge. Three men were waiting in front of it. One
of them I knew by sight as the second Honourable Farnsworth-Jones. I imagined the other two were the Scottish
servants, Angus and Malcolm. They were the tallest, thin-
nest men I'd ever seen. Both had red hair and red beards
and red faces. And both were wearing skirts—short,
pleated red-and-green ones—that stopped above their
big, red knees. Above the skirts they wore brown tweed
jackets and below them thick red-and-blue stockings.
Thanks to Sir Walter Scott I knew these were Scottish
costumes and that the skirts were called kilts. I'd never
seen the Scotsmen in town, though Esther had once described them to me. She hadn't said one word about them
wearing skirts, so I guessed they dressed like men, not
ladies, when they had to leave the castle. That would have
been wise of them.

One of the Scots hauled me down from the wagon as if I had no bulk to me at all, while Mr. Alfred very gently helped Sarah Jane to the ground like she'd bust if she lit hard. I was gratified to see that he took such good care of her. He must be taken with her, then.

Mr. Alfred introduced us to his brother, who introduced us to the two Scots. They both bowed a bit and grumbled something I didn't catch. Where the honourables talked high through their noses, the Scots talked low, growling in their throats. They all seemed to understand each other well, though.

After we had met everyone, Sarah Jane and I followed the two honourables and Mr. Angus over the drawbridge and into the castle to start our grand tour. Mr. Malcolm went to start making tea in the ranch house. We walked around the great hall, through the pantries, and across the big kitchen where a cook could roast a steer whole in the fireplace. We climbed up narrow stairs single file to see the smaller rooms above them, and then up more steep steps to the third and fourth stories.

I didn't take to all that rock. How our footsteps rang gloomily on the stone floors! How cold and breezy it was, with the prairie winds blowing in through the little glass-less windows that were just wide enough to shoot arrows through in the old days. It was very dim inside the castle, though it was daylight outside. If there had been any furniture, I would surely have fallen over it. The whole place was as bare as the big, unused hotel ballroom in Chicago I'd once peeked into when Uncle Julius wasn't looking.

At the very top of the castle I leaned over what the Honourable Alfred called a battlement. The height made me feel dizzy. A gust of wind blew my hat off my head, and it would have landed in the moat if there had been one.

By the time we all came back down to the great hall, I'd made up my mind that I wouldn't truly want to live in the Farnsworth-Jones castle even with lots of comfortable furniture. It wasn't only that the castle was grim and drafty—there was that ghost. I kept my eyes and ears peeled but didn't see her or hear one wail.

His voice echoing all around, Mr. Albert said, "We will be refurbishing the old place with some family furnishings. We've recently sent to England for them and they should be here and installed by spring, when we intend to have a modest gathering of our friends out here, friends from England, that is."

Because I was curious, I asked, "Was it hard getting your castle up. It must have an awful lot of rocks in it."

"Thousands, my dear," said Mr. Albert, who seemed to like my question. "However, they were designated by number as to where they were to go, and our father had sent us a blueprint to work from."

"And you didn't have any pieces left over at all?"

"Nary a one. We all worked on the project, using our muscles as well as our minds. With the capable help of Mr. Potter from Goldendale and some workmen he hired for us from nearby Heberville, the whole thing progressed splendidly. When it is furnished, we shall move in and become true farmers, devoting our time and energies to raising Scottish cattle, merino sheep, and blooded horses." Now he looked at me and asked, "Well, my gel, what do you think of our little palace on the plains?"

Telling the pure truth, I said, "I never saw anything in my whole life like it before in Chicago or anywhere else."

He smiled and said, "Come along then and take tea with us in the ranch house."

After I picked up my hat and learned from Mr. Angus that they didn't dig a moat because there wasn't enough water for one, Sarah Jane and I had tea with the two honourables in their wooden ranch house. After the castle, that was a pretty ordinary building. The furniture was made of plain old American golden oak like most folks'. It had the same kind of chairs and tables and kerosene lamps Judge Garway had, and even some of the same pictures on the wall. I figured the honourables had bought it lock, stock, and barrel from the ranch's former owner.

If the house was ordinary, the tea sure wasn't. I'd been to teas that Aunt Rhoda had taken me to so that I could learn etiquette, but this wasn't like those Chicago ones. The teapot looked to be solid silver. The china cups and saucers were very thin and had gold all over them and golden shields in the middle. The food was wonderful. Mr. Malcolm could sure cook. There were little spicy-tasting sandwiches on white bread, smoked salmon, chocolate biscuits, hot scones and marmalade, and melt-in-the-mouth Scotch shortbread. Even their tea tasted better than most tea did. Mr. Albert said it was because they warmed the pot first, which was something to remember.

I could see that Sarah Jane was impressed by the tea, too, and ate very daintily. She kept looking over at me and frowned once when I stretched out my hand for a third chocolate biscuit. I took the biscuit because I already had my fingers on it but didn't take thirds of anything else —though I was invited to by Mr. Albert. When she said it was a "delightful and delicious repast," I politely added, "Likewise," which was what Uncle Julius often said.

After we'd eaten, Mr. Alfred said he thought it was time to return to Goldendale. He wanted to leave before twilight so he could still see the ruts in the road.

I asked, "Will we go back the same way we came?" If he said yes, I planned to stuff a scone into my pocket to give me strength for the dull trip home.

Mr. Alfred turned to ask my sister, "Would you like to take a different route, Miss Carpenter? There's an alternate way through the hamlet of Heberville."

Heberville! That's where the courthouse was going up.

Because I was also named Miss Carpenter and he hadn't definitely said Miss Sarah Jane, I answered before he finished. "You bet!" Here was my chance to see Goldendale's rival for the county seat.

After curtseying to everybody, even though Mr. Angus looked surprised at my knowing the right thing to do, we got back up into Mr. Alfred's wagon. This time we jolted off north by west, not due west as before.

Some time later we saw a church spire ahead, which let me know a town was there. Heberville.

I looked it over carefully as we went down its main street, called Market Street. I took note of the buildings. Many were of precut lumber, too, like Goldendale's. I recognized a number of them as being the same as the judge's house and the Potter place, model 42-A. You couldn't miss the courthouse between the city hall and the jail. The frame was up, and it had some of the siding on it. It was the same as Goldendale's firehouse and had lots of room. Yes, the judge would like one just like it.

I sighed and glanced over at the Honourable Alfred. He was busy talking into Sarah Jane's ear as she sat beside him, looking straight ahead. He was talking low, so I couldn't hear what he was saying, but I could guess. Yes, he was smitten with her. He had looked glassy-eyed at her over the chocolate biscuits a couple of times. I'd seen that look

on men's faces before when they got to gawking at my
sister.

We got home to Goldendale before dark and arrived
in time to give the judge the Sunday-night supper I hated
and he loved—sardines, cheese, and sliced onions. While
I was carefully opening a sardine tin, I asked Sarah Jane,
"Are you going out again with Mr. Alfred?"

As she sliced an onion, she sniffled. "Yes, he's asked me
to a dance Saturday evening at a lodge hall in Heberville.
He says he likes to waltz. And I intend to see to it that
you don't accompany me when I go out again!" And once
more she sniffled. Was it the onion or was it still grief?

Before school started the next day, I gave Esther and
Violet a complete description of my visit to the Englishmen's castle. They were big-eyed and openmouthed, but
like true friends, they weren't one bit jealous. They didn't
act like Stump Wood, who came up to us under our
cottonwood and said, mean-eyed, "I spotted you yesterday sashaying around with one of those jaspers from
England, Melinda. I suppose because you hail from fancy
Chicago you and your sister are stuck on him. Americans
aren't good enough for you, huh?"

After he shoved his hands into his pockets and slouched
off to join a bunch of his friends a distance away, Violet
told me, "Don't you mind him, Melinda. He's jealous
because you saw the castle and he never did."

"Violet, I don't care what Stump thinks. I just wish Sarah Jane would get stuck on the Honourable Alfred. Maybe she will. She's going out with him again Saturday."

Esther now touched my arm. "Melinda, I've asked Violet already. Can you come to my house and have a *Shabbes* supper with us Friday night? Mama asked me to ask you."

"What does your papa say?"

"He says fine. He's over being mad at you. Mr. Bauman, the druggist, is coming, and so is our friend Dr. Harmon."

I thought of Dr. Harmon, who might ask me about my swoon. Yet I did want to go, so if he asked me, I'd say I'd had a bilious attack because of something I'd eaten. I'd ask Sarah Jane if I could go, but I was pretty sure she'd let me.

That afternoon I did ask and she said it was fine with her as long as I behaved, which I promised faithfully.

The rest of the week went by as usual. I went to school and dogcatched and dog hauled and was dog hauled. The only interesting thing to happen was that a big box arrived from Chicago with our winter duds—capes and coats, flannel nightgowns, and long, woolen unmentionables.

Oh, but I was excited when Friday rolled around. Esther had told us that day at school to doll up a bit and be sure and show up at her house before sunset. She said it was important to be on time for the Sabbath supper. Sunset was important because the Sabbath started when it grew dark.

Violet and I met in front of the Mittelman store and looked each other over carefully for clean necks and fingernails. Violet and I both had our hair in long curls. She wore mustard-yellow taffeta and I wore my rose plush dress that had just arrived from Chicago.

We walked around to the rear of the store and knocked on the back door, which was the Mittelmans' front door. Esther let us inside. She had a big blue bow in her hair and wore a pale blue silk dress. My, but we were all elegant tonight! Esther said, "Come on in. The others are already here."

We went through her parlor into the dining room so fast I didn't even see it clearly. The dining-room table was covered with a white cloth and had a vase of yellow and red prairie wild flowers on it. There were also four white candles in silver candlesticks. Near them was a glass decanter of dark wine and a tall silver cup. Two loaves of bread peeked out from under an embroidered cloth.

Esther said, "Sit down in the empty seats."

I looked around and saw that the three Mittelman sons, Mr. Bauman, and the doctor were already seated. I figured the two empty chairs at one end of the table were for her parents, so I scooted to one of the three empty ones along the sides and sat next to Joshua Mittelman. Esther sat beside me in the other chair, and Violet across from us, between Dr. Harmon and Ben.

Mrs. Mittelman was sure dressed up tonight. She had on a white silk dress, a gold-and-garnet necklace and earbobs, and over her head a scarf of white silk lace. All of the men wore dark suits and had small, round, black caps on top of their heads.

Mr. Mittelman sat down, but not his wife. I watched as she struck a match and lit the four candles. Then she waved her hands over them three times and put her palms over her eyes. She said aloud, "Blessed art thou, O Lord our God, King of the Universe, who has sanctified us to kindle the Sabbath lights."

As her mother remained silent with her hands over her eyes, Esther whispered to me, "There's a candle for each of us kids."

Mr. Mittelman got up now. He walked around the table, touched the heads of each of his sons, and said over each, "May God make thee like Ephraim and Manasseh." Then he came to Esther and did the same thing, saying, "May God make thee like Sarah, Rebecca, Rachel, and Leah."

When he came back to the table, he poured wine out of the decanter into the silver goblet and chanted a short song in a foreign language.

Esther whispered to me again, "Papa's praying, praising Mama's goodness in Hebrew. She's a queen tonight. All Jewish mothers are at the Shabbes supper."

Next, Mr. Mittelman broke a loaf of bread into pieces and sent one piece after another down the table to each person there. After that he gave the silver cup first to his wife, who took a sip, then passed it to the person next to her, who sipped and passed it on. When it came to me, I took a sip of the sweet wine that tasted like raisins, and then gave the cup to Esther who sipped and sent it on again. After everyone had taken a drink, Mr. Mittelman sipped, too. The Mittelmans sang together in Hebrew, and then supper was served by Esther and her mother.

It was delicious. We had noodles in chicken broth, a spicy stuffed pickled fish, roast chicken, carrots in honey, and the rest of the bread. Then we had coffee cake, a dessert made out of canned figs, and tea with lemon and sugar.

When supper was over, Mr. Mittelman smiled at Violet, Esther, and me as we got up and went into the parlor. He hadn't once mentioned the word *minyan*, and Dr. Harmon hadn't said anything about my swooning.

As we sat on the sofa, I told Esther how much I'd liked being their guest.

She smiled as she said, "Melinda, do you remember what we sang just before supper?"

"Uh-huh, I remember the melody, even if I didn't understand a word of it."

"It was about angels. We were singing, 'Welcome to you, O ministering angels, may your coming be in peace, may you bless us with peace, and may you depart in peace.' That's what families sing when the father comes home from the temple to the Sabbath supper."

I nodded. I thought it was just fine that angels were thanked and welcomed in some places on Friday nights, not just on Christmas or Easter, which was when most people considered angels in their thoughts.

Violet said, "But there isn't any temple for your pa to come home from, Esther."

Esther nodded. "And not even a *minyan*. Mama won't cut any yard goods tomorrow or even cook until sundown because of the day's being holy, but Papa and my brothers will work in the store all the same. We have to stay open on Saturday, the busiest day of the week. Our religion lets people work on the Sabbath day if they have to in order to make a living. Someday Papa will be able to hire men who aren't Jewish to work for him on Saturdays, but right now he can't afford the money for wages. My brothers don't get paid."

I asked, "Hey, could you stay open Sundays instead?"

Esther shook her head. "No, Goldendale has a city law against stores being open. Papa says most places in America have laws like that about Sunday."

Now that I'd had time to think about that, I realized I'd asked a stupid question. I told Violet, "That's true.

You can go to church or to a cafe or a park or saloon in Chicago, but you can't buy a can of peaches or a new hat. Saloons are open here and so is the hotel, but not much else."

Esther went on. "Yes. Mama and I will rest tomorrow. She gave me permission to come out last Saturday when you needed me to help you trap the Honourable Mr. Alfred. She thought you needed me to help find Edward Gideon. I told her a white lie in a good cause."

"Thank you, Esther. You are a true-blue pal, you know!"

❦9❧
Winter and Spring

Sarah Jane stepped out with the Honourable Alfred on either Friday or Saturday night for the next couple of weeks, but she didn't tell me what she thought of him or even if she was having a good time. I started to ask her once, and she wouldn't even reply but only looked mournfully out the kitchen window. If she enjoyed being squired by an honourable, she sure didn't show it by being bright and sunny around the house. Well, maybe that was because of the changing weather. First it was rainy, then a few weeks later, snowy. It finally got so cold I couldn't do as much traipsing about with Esther and Violet as I used to do. I usually went out-of-doors only to dogcatch Edward Gideon, and that job got harder in bad weather because he seemed to struggle more. Sometimes when the wind blew in from the snow-covered prairie or down from the mountains, I would have sworn it was below zero, the way it got in Chicago when Lake Erie froze. The judge said it wasn't that cold but just my "powerful child's imagination at work."

Occasionally I'd spot Mr. Potter on Main Street in his wagon. It seemed that he always looked away from me. I know once I got him in my view I looked away from him. As for Mrs. Potter, I never once saw her, not even in Mittelman's Emporium. I saw blanket-wearing Indians in tall cowboy hats and moccasins, prospectors with long beards down from the hills, and everybody else in town in there, but not Mrs. Potter. When I asked about her, Mrs. Mittelman said she was a true homebody.

Sarah Jane and I kept in touch with Aunt Rhoda and Uncle Julius by letter every week, and I thought perhaps we'd go back to Chicago for the Christmas holidays. Sarah Jane was going to business school two nights a week and by now had enough money for train tickets; but when I asked her about going, she only gave me one of her drooping looks and went to play something melancholy on the piano.

Christmas wasn't much fun. We spent it quietly with Judge Garway. He gave us each little gold nuggets on chains, and we gave him a sardonyx stickpin. I gave Sarah Jane a twelve-inch-long, jet-headed hatpin, half for an ornament and half for protection, and she gave me bright red earmuffs. Edward Gideon got the biggest, meatiest bone I could buy at the butcher's as a present from all of us. He chewed on it for days, rattling it around on the closed-in back porch where he lived when he was home. Snow on the ground or falling from the sky didn't keep him from roaming.

I spent New Year's Eve alone. Edward Gideon jumped the fence at six o'clock, the Honourable Alfred called for Sarah Jane in a sleigh at seven to take her to supper at the Pronghorn Hotel and then to a vaudeville show in the just-built opera house, and the judge went to a party given by a lawyer friend. I sat in the parlor reading by lamplight until I fell sound asleep on the sofa and was awakened by Sarah Jane coming home.

There wasn't much to say for the month of January, 1894, except that Sarah Jane started being courted by two of Goldendale's bachelor lawyers, a whiskery one and a bald one, as well as by Mr. Alfred. She didn't seem to be taking greatly to any one of them, but at least she was keeping her promise to me by going out.

One night early in February, Sarah Jane came blowing into the house in a flurry of snow after going out with the Honourable Alfred. As I helped her out of her long, heavy ulster and she unwound a scarf from around her head, she told me in a funny, flat voice, "I know this will disappoint you, Melinda, but I will not be going out with Mr. Farnsworth-Jones anymore."

"Did he mash you?"

"No, he'd hinted before at my becoming the mistress of his manor, but tonight he went further. He showed me a piece of jewelry he had in his pocket. It was an old brooch set with diamonds. He said it had belonged to his mother. He was mentioning marriage. I told him I would not consider marrying any man, but that I was greatly flattered at the suggestion."

"What did he say?"

"Good-bye, more or less. He asked if my refusal was due to his having cheated at whist and being sent away by his father. I told him no, I just did not want to marry. I will not see him again. The day a lady refuses to marry a man is usually the final time she sees him. Men do understand this. Good night, Melinda." And up she went to bed, leaving me holding her cold, damp coat, thinking of the Honourable Alfred who had been a card cheater. Well, now I knew the bad thing he had done.

I was a card cheater, too. So was every kid I knew.

As I hung up the coat to dry, I considered Mr. Albert. What about *him* and Sarah Jane? After thinking for a time, I decided I didn't want to take a hand in his case. He hadn't shown a lot of interest in her, and when he heard she didn't want his brother, he might get the idea she didn't want either one of them. It hadn't been easy getting her involved with the Honourable Alfred. She'd seen through my scheme then, so she'd be sure to see through anything I tried to do about the Honourable Albert, too.

I sighed. Oh, well, I'd never live in the castle, but there were still those two lawyers here in Goldendale.

It didn't snow on Valentine's Day. The sun shown so brightly on the snow it made my eyes hurt as I walked to school. I exchanged hand-drawn valentines with Esther and Violet and that was that.

That evening we all went to bed early. Sarah Jane had gone up quietly, taking a novel with her. The judge had gone grumpily because he'd just read in the paper that the state legislature had postponed deciding where to put the seat of the new county. The judge hated suspense.

I was the last to go upstairs. While I was sitting on my bed brushing my hair to get some snarls out of it, I heard a thump on the front porch just below my window. Then I heard a deep barking that I knew belonged to Edward Gideon. He was the only dog in town that barked like a ship's foghorn on Lake Erie. But what was he doing home at this hour? It had to be because he'd followed somebody here from town. Could it be a burglar?

Thinking of burglars, I got up off the bed and ran to look out my window. What I saw in the bright moon-light made me gasp. Stump Wood! Stump Wood, his long legs pumping, was racing lickety-split down the walkway and through the open gate. He slammed the gate shut a split second before Edward Gideon got through. By the time the dog backed off and took a running leap over the gate, Stump was on his bicycle wheeling fast as he could down a hard-packed snow track in the street. Stump made fine time, but Edward Gideon didn't. His big legs kept stumbling. He'd get up, run, then fall again into the snow. He kept picking himself up, shaking himself free of snow, then go on again. Holding my breath, I watched the two of them out of sight down Cedar Street and onto Main.

What was Stump doing on our front porch? I had heard Stump's thump! Holding my lamp, I went out into the hallway to find the judge and my sister in dressing gowns, looking worried.

Judge Garway said, "I would have sworn I heard my dog barking. Do you suppose he sneaks back here some nights and I've never known it?"

I said, "It was him. He came back here chasing somebody riding on a bicycle."

"A bicycle in the snow? Who'd do such a thing?" asked Sarah Jane.

"Somebody I know from school. He rides it in the ruts wagons make. I saw him out my window. He came to play a prank on me, I bet. He hates me." Oh, how I hoped it wasn't another one of his firecrackers, the long-fuse kind, lit to go off on the front porch any second now.

I said, "I'll go down and see that everything's all right on the porch. You can go back to bed."

The judge mumbled, "All right. Call me if it's a bomb. Otherwise, don't call me."

I nodded. He and I had both read in the newspaper recently about revolutionaries in Russia who were throwing bombs at people they didn't like. I went downstairs and peered through the glass-paneled front door. Yes, there was something on the porch, but it wasn't shaped like a firecracker. It was cone shaped, with white stuff on one end. I unlocked the door, went out, picked the object up, and took it inside. It was a cone of paper, red paper and white paper lace. I knew what it was at once —a store-bought valentine from Mittelman's.

On the outside of the cone was my name written in pencil. I put down the lamp and opened the valentine. It was heart shaped, with a fat, pink cupid on it aiming an arrow at another fat cupid. Under them were the words "your secret admirer," but no name. Stump? Stump Wood admired *me?* I was speechless with amazement. A sudden rush of warmth flowed all over me, feet to head, and I felt dizzy. What a secret from such a secret admirer! I put the valentine into the deep pocket of my dressing gown, relocked the door, took the lamp, and went upstairs.

Sarah Jane's voice floated out to me from her room. "Was everything all right, Melinda?"

"Yes, he was only making a noise. It wasn't anything at all to worry about. The door's locked and the gate's shut."

Thrilled, I looked at the valentine in my room before hiding it in my copy of *The Three Musketeers*. No, I wouldn't tell Violet or Esther. I'd pretend that I hadn't even seen Stump come to my house, and watch him tomorrow to see how he'd act toward me. I figured he'd be meaner to me than ever, but now I knew how he really felt. It made me feel sort of powerful—to be admired. This must be how ladies felt when they were being courted. He had a crush on me. I didn't have one on him, but all at once I thought I understood my sister better. There could be something to say for love.

The next day Stump was just as mean as I figured he'd be. He was almost as ornery as Gar, who'd been snowbound on his farm for almost a whole month. Gar didn't want to be in school now either, but he had to since the road from his place to town was clear of drifts. He sat with his brother, both of them glowering at everybody and only grunting when Miss Hawkins called on them.

Early spring was mostly wet, and warm enough to melt the snow so the creek rose and flooded the schoolyard. We waded to the schoolhouse for a week. At first

I'd hoped Stump would offer to carry me, but he never did. He let me get my feet wet like everybody else. Now and then, though, I'd catch his dark eyes looking at me over the top of a book when he thought I wasn't looking. I'd taken careful note that I was the only girl he ever gawked at. That pleased me.

After all of the snow was gone and the creek went down, things began to pick up in Goldendale, even if they didn't pick up at the judge's house.

Each time I passed the depot hunting for Edward Gideon, I seemed to see another big pile of crates waiting to be carted off. They were all marked for Farnsworth-Jones, Goldendale, Colorado, U.S.A., and they all came from London, England. Remembering what the honourables said about furnishing their castle, I figured these were crates of furniture. Some of them were big enough to hold pianos. So the Englishmen were about to move into their castle.

I also found out from Esther that the honourables were buying out her folks' store of food supplies—tea and biscuits, wine and whiskey. I was sure they were stocking up for the English guests they'd talked about last fall. Mr. Mittelman said they were buying as if they expected their castle to be besieged by some enemy for months at a time. Well, I wished I could go to the house party to see how the castle looked with furniture in it, but I knew that neither Sarah Jane nor I would be invited. She had been

dead right about the Honourable Alfred. He'd never once
darkened the judge's door since she had refused his
brooch.

April brought some more excitement to Goldendale.
One Monday morning Esther, who lived nearest to the
depot, came running up to Violet and me before school
hollering, "Come see what's on the railroad tracks!"

As we ran after her, she yelled, "It's cars, special ones.
And people are getting out of them."

Special railroad cars? Could it be a circus?

When we got to the depot, we joined a crowd of
people staring at nine railroad cars on a siding. There were
five shiny, elegant green, blue, and maroon private cars.
Four were wooden-sided cattle cars. Men whom I'd never
set eyes on before kept going into and coming out of the
fancy cars. Then both of the honourables stepped down
out of the darkest green one. Mr. Potter was with them,
nodding and talking. Finally he walked off with some
other men toward the cattle cars.

Now I spotted Mr. Alfred's wagon and watched as he
and five men piled into it and drove off. Then came
Angus, driving a big wagon rented from the livery stable.
He took away nine more galoots. Six more left in another
rented wagon driven by Malcolm. That left only the
Honourable Albert and Mr. Potter, who were standing

together in front of the cattle cars, acting as if they were waiting.

Esther tugged at my arm. "We better get back to school before Miss Hawkins rings her bell."

Stump had heard her and told us, "You girls can go on back, but not me. I'm gonna hang around here and see what's in the cow cars."

I said, "You better not. You'll get in trouble."

"I don't care, Melindy."

Violet told him, "Suit yourself, stupid," and she, Esther, and I left with almost all of the other kids.

I'd wanted to know what was in the cattle cars, too, because I hadn't heard one single *moo* from them, but I had to leave. On our way back to school I told Esther and Violet who I thought the men in the wagons were—the Englishmen the honourables had invited to their house party. I also told them why the Englishmen traveled in private cars. Everybody in Chicago knew that that was the finest way of all for rich folks to get around. But none of us could figure out why they would fetch along ugly, old cattle cars.

"Stump'll find out," I said. "He'll tell us what he saw. He likes to be important. All we have to do is ask him nicely."

We had to wait, though, because he didn't appear until lunchtime; then Miss Hawkins caught him first and dragged him and the two boys who were with him into the schoolhouse for a ten-minute tongue-lashing. After she let Stump go, he came out to our cottonwood tree and leaned against it, grinning.

I asked, "Stump, what was in the cattle cars?"

He teased me, of course. "Not cows like you think."

I shot back at him, "What was it, then? Bulls?"

"Nope, guess again."

"Elephants?" asked Esther in disgust.

"Nope. Horses and dogs. There was twenty horses and a whole bunch of dogs, white-and-brown, flop-eared ones." He grinned at me. "It's a good thing your big dog was asleep in the storeroom of the Drover's Paradise Saloon when they unloaded the dogs. They tied the horses in a long string, and one of those Englishmen who set up the castle rode the lead one. Fine looking horses, too. Big, long-legged, brown-and-black ones, nary a pinto. They put the dogs in two cages that came off of the cattle cars, and old Mr. Potter fetched them along in his wagon behind all the horses. He and the Englishman had got 'em into the cages, but it wasn't easy dealing with so many dogs. Them animals made a heckuva lot of uproar."

I asked, "How many dogs?"

"I dunno. A dozen or more."

I said nicely, "Thank you for telling us." Then I added, "I'm glad they didn't let the dogs loose in town. There are enough dogs here already. Did you say you saw my dog in the Drover's Paradise Saloon?"

"Yep. I stopped by there with a friend of mine whose pa is the bartender."

I wanted to groan. That was the one saloon in Goldendale where I got snapped at for asking about the judge's dog. Well, I'd just have to go there, no matter what.

I comforted myself with the thought that when I got Edward Gideon out of there and took him home, I'd have some interesting news to tell Sarah Jane. Hearing about the private cars and horses and dogs could perk her up.

It didn't, though. I found her using the feather duster in the parlor. She went right on dusting as I told her about the new arrivals. All she said was, "That's interesting, isn't it?" and flicked a cobweb off a picture frame. She didn't seem to care one bit about the goings-on at the castle.

Sarah Jane appeared to me to be drooping even more now that spring had come. She'd lost some weight, and she didn't ever laugh. She took the molasses-and-sulphur spring tonic Aunt Rhoda said we should both take, but it didn't seem to do her much good. Her skin was so pale you could almost see through it, and her hair had lost some of its yellow shine. She'd stopped going out with the lawyers and didn't even go downtown herself to buy supplies. Instead, she called in orders on the telephone and had them delivered to the house. Joshua Mittelman came there lots of times with boxes of groceries.

I worried about my sister. It wasn't as if I didn't know what ailed her. It was that cussed Edgar Everett. I saw now that lovesickness was a real illness. What could I do to help her?

That Saturday night Judge Garway gave a party in honor of a young lawyer friend of his who'd just won his first case in court. It was a supper party, and I helped Sarah Jane. I brought the food to the table and served the guests because my sister told me she wanted to stay in the kitchen. Two of the guests were the lawyers who had squired her about, and she didn't want them to see her. So I was the waitress.

The judge passed around bottles of whiskey and wine all evening. As I brought in the coffee and apple-pie-and-cheese dessert, I heard him telling stories about the old days when Colorado was still a territory, not yet a state. Some of his tales were exciting, like the one about the stagecoach with lots of money aboard disappearing into thin air in Ute Canyon. Others, like the one about a miner friend who froze to death in a blizzard, were sad. Just as I was setting down the last cup of coffee on my tray, I heard him say, "You know, gentlemen, a good bit of what I've just told you is somewhat exaggerated, but the traveling house I am now going to tell you about is fact."

"A traveling house?" asked a young lawyer.

Judge Garway lit a cheroot, leaned back in his chair,

and said with a laugh, "As you know, when a man files for a homestead with the federal government, he has to prove that he does a certain amount of improvements on it to keep legal hold of the land. One way to do this is to put up a building on it. Doing that, of course, takes time and money—something a lot of homesteaders don't have. Well, one group of homesteaders found a way around this. An enterprising galoot of considerable slickness made himself a special house that could be put on wheels and set down anywhere a team of horses hauled it. He rented the house out by the week.

"When a homesteader knew the inspectors were due to come to his homestead looking for improvements, he could hire the slicker and his house. After it was off its wheels and just sitting on the prairie, it looked like it had been built there. When the inspectors saw it, they would give their approval to the homesteader for another year and leave. Once they were out of sight, back went the house onto its wheels, and it would be hauled to the next homesteader who had rented it. That little house went all over the state hoodwinking inspectors until it plumb fell apart from its traveling."

How the lawyers laughed! I didn't, though, because I don't like crooked doings.

The party went on downstairs, but Sarah Jane and I went up to bed after we finished cleaning up the kitchen.

I fell asleep immediately but woke up when I heard the

company leaving. I could tell from the men's voices that they'd had plenty of the judge's whiskey and wine. They were very loud. My bedroom window was open, and I got up to shut their noise out. Just as I was ready to pull the window down, I heard one man say, "Didn't we have a dandy time tonight?"

"We sure did," said another. "You'd never guess the judge is upset that Heberville will probably be the county seat because of their courthouse. That's what they're saying in Denver. The judge'll be getting the bad news any day now."

A third voice put in, "Maybe we ought to do something to tickle the judge's chin whiskers."

A fourth man guffawed. "I bet I know what you've got in mind, Luke."

I didn't know and I didn't care. I closed my mind to what I'd heard about the judge's chin whiskers and climbed back into bed. I had more important things on my mind. Earlier I'd heard Sarah Jane crying in her room while they were all drinking and having a good time below. She wasn't getting over Edgar Everett Potter III. She was pining and making herself sick. It was time for me to take a hand again!

I'd had a thought come to me, but first of all I needed to find that awful letter and reread it to be absolutely sure of what was written in it. I thought I knew where it was

—in her jewel box with the pearl necklace she was to wear as a bride and the amethyst ring *he* had given her.

I did find the letter there the next morning after she went off to church. Fibbing, I told her I felt a cold coming on and that I'd like to stay home to nip it in the bud. I unfolded the letter and read it again. Then I took it down to the judge, who was sitting in his study looking peaked and drinking lots of black coffee.

I told him, "I need a good, clear opinion on something, sir."

He muttered, "I'm not sure you came to the right man this morning, Melinda."

Now I handed him the letter and asked, "Please read this and tell me what you think of it."

He took it and read it, not just once but three times, pulling at his beard each time he got to the bad part. At last he told me, "If this were a legal matter, I would ask for clarification. It seems quite odd to me that a young man should marry a girl because in his opinion she is lonely."

"That's what I think, and I'm sure that's what Sarah Jane thinks, too. That's why she's so sad. She loves the galoot."

"I see." He leaned back. "What part have you played in all this?"

"I sent some telegrams." I told him what was in them,

then added, "She told me to send whatever I thought was right. I told her what I sent and she didn't say I did wrong. I was only protecting her."

He shook his head very slowly and said, "You certainly took a lot on your young shoulders, didn't you? You should have let your sister get in touch with young Potter and your family in Illinois herself. It may seem to you that you helped her, but in fact I would say that you didn't. Melinda, people who are always protected never become strong themselves. People who are always protecting others can get strong, but they can also get danged weary. It's not good either way. You were hasty. It is never wise to be hasty. I think you have done your sister a disservice, though you had good intentions; perhaps you have done a disservice to Mr. Potter, too."

"To *him?*"

"Perhaps. He should know what he's done, don't you think? He deserves a chance to justify himself in his parents' eyes, at least. No wonder his father has looked so down-in-the-mouth these last months since you arrived here." The judge handed the letter back to me.

"Thank you, sir. You've helped me a lot. You give good advice."

"Have I? Are you sure?"

"Yes, indeed."

I marched back upstairs, put the letter back into the jewel box, and sat down at my little table with paper, pen, and ink. In my best and clearest handwriting I wrote to Edgar Everett Potter III, dating my letter and writing Goldendale, Colorado, in the upper right-hand corner.

Dear sir,
   Remember me? I'm Sarah Jane's little sister, Melinda. She and I are still in Goldendale.
   When she read your letter last fall, I read it, too. I want to tell you about that letter. Sarah Jane was never lonesome in her whole life, but you kept writing the word lonely *over and over. I do not think you should have hurt her in her pride by telling her you wanted to marry her out of pity.*
   I want to tell you, too, that I sent you that telegram about her eloping with a train conductor on the way here. It was a fib. She hasn't married anybody, though I know she's been asked to here. She's working for Judge Garway as his housekeeper. I am his dogcatcher.
   I think you should send an apology to my sister. I'm not letting her or anybody else know I am writing this to you. She'd stop me if she knew. This is Judge Garway's address, 48 Cedar Street.
                 Very truly yours,
                 Melinda Albertine Carpenter

I stuffed the letter into an envelope, addressed it to him, sealed it, and put a stamp on it. Then I went out with

Edward Gideon's leash. First I'd mail the letter at the mailbox outside the post office, then I'd hunt down the judge's dog.

After I posted the letter, I paused for a moment, wondering if I should have mentioned anything about love at first sight being unreliable. But then I decided I wasn't so sure about love matters as I once was. Sarah Jane wasn't getting over him. Love at first sight could be real and last longer than I thought, but it could be perilous, too. Look at Romeo and Juliet. They had been smitten with each other right off. But look at how sadly their romance had ended. Romeo and Juliet had been hasty!

·IO·
Somewhat More
Than I Had Expected

That was Sunday. Another week of school lay ahead of me.

Each day after school when I'd collared Edward Gideon somewhere or other, Violet, Esther, and I walked to the depot with him to see if the Englishmen's cars had left yet. They hadn't. They were still there, being looked after by a watchman sitting on the platform above them. I figured he'd been hired by Mr. Potter to keep people out of the private cars. Plenty of folks—me for one— would have liked to look inside them, but we didn't dare go up close or we'd get yelled at to get away.

On my way back to the judge's with Edward Gideon Friday afternoon, he and I collided with Dr. Harmon, who was coming out of Bauman's drugstore. He was carrying his black doctor's bag, and I thought he looked weary.

As I pulled Edward Gideon away from him, the doctor asked me the question I'd been worried he'd ask me ever since last fall. "Have you had any fainting spells lately?"

I had been hoping he would have forgotten all about that by now. He must have a very good memory, or I'd pulled a remarkable fainting spell.

"Oh, no," I replied, then hesitated. Rather than have him always think I was a puny weakling, I decided to tell the truth. "I didn't really have that one. It wasn't a real swoon. I only did it to get noticed."

"Noticed?" His bristly gray eyebrows rose up.

"Uh-huh. Noticed by the Honourable Alfred Farnsworth-Jones."

"My lord, child, you could have been killed by his team of horses. I saw what happened. Don't do that sort of fool thing ever again! Besides, aren't you a bit young for him?"

"I didn't do it so he'd notice me. I did it for my sister, Sarah Jane."

He nodded. "Yes, the tall, pale beauty I see in church."

"That's her. She sure is pale, but it isn't anything you doctors can help with. She's sick from love."

"You're right. Medical men can't cure that. I trust it isn't Alfred Farnsworth-Jones?"

"Nope, not him. She said no to his proposal."

He gave me a sharp look, then said, "That castle of his is a wild place right now, no place for a lady. I just came from there. I attended somebody who said he was an earl. He'd jumped off a battlement into a load of hay. He was pretty liquored up."

"Are all the guests still out there?"

He nodded. "Indeed they are—carousing. The party goes on day and night, so far as I can tell. I hope I'm not called out there again. One of those tall Scots was hammering on my door at six this morning about the leaping earl. Well, I'm going to bed, if my patients will let me." He reached into his coat pocket and pulled out a big, brown bottle and said, "This is for me. It's beef wine, corn whiskey, and peppermint. My good friend, Jake Bauman, makes it up for me special. He calls it Bauman's Best Bitters. It keeps me going. The life of a frontier doctor can be strenuous for a man my age. Adults need comforting tonics at times. Say, are you taking any sulphur and molasses? You look a bit peaked."

"Yes, I never miss a day. If I look peaked, it's because I fret over my sister."

He shook his head and said, "Well, good-bye, my dear. Don't be fainting anymore. I don't approve." And off he went after putting the bottle back into his pocket and patting Edward Gideon on the head.

That night Sarah Jane gave a piano recital for Judge

Garway and some of his lawyer friends and their wives.
I served coffee and cakes. On Saturday I dog-sat Edward
Gideon, as usual. He was friskier and stronger because it
was springtime and hauled me more than I pulled him.

Because the judge said it was very warm for late April,
we all rested after church on Sunday. That evening Sarah
Jane and I were glum over supper, and the judge was even
glummer. He had just about given up hope of Goldendale
becoming the county seat because Heberville's courthouse, which had been left unfinished during the winter
months, was finally completed.

How tired I was of hearing about the county splitting
in two and of Heberville's courthouse. I was tired of
school, of hunting Great Dane dogs, of odd-behaving
Englishmen, and especially of Edgar Everett Potter III,
who could have written back to Sarah Jane or me by now
but hadn't. I was tired of everything—even of Stump's
staring at me at school. I guess I had a case of spring fever,
all right. I took twice as much molasses and sulphur that
night before I went to bed because I felt so strange.

I slept strangely, too, having one little dream after
another. One was a nightmare that made me open my eyes
in fright, thinking somebody was opening my bedroom
door very slowly, making it groan and squeak. I looked
at my door. No, it wasn't opening. Yet I could hear
noises, and they were real, creaking ones.

I got up, went to my wide-open window, and looked out onto Cedar Street. Was it Stump Wood again? What was he up to now? No, I didn't see a soul in the light of a half moon. But I still heard squeakings and creakings. Then I heard men's voices. Leaning out as far as I could, I looked toward Main Street at the end of Cedar.

Great, thumping Jehoshaphat! I couldn't believe my eyes. I rubbed them and looked again, but it was still there. There was a building in the middle of Main Street where no building ought to be. And not only that, it was *moving!* I crawled out onto the porch roof for a better view. From there I could see that the building was being pulled slowly along by a team of mules with men on horseback riding alongside. I crawled back inside and got the judge's sister's opera glasses from a dresser drawer, went back onto the roof, and looked again. The building was on top of some sort of sledge with wheels on it, and the whole thing was being pulled down the street by the mule team.

I got back into my room, put on my wrapper and slippers, and went to knock on the judge's bedroom door.

"Who is it?" he asked sleepily.

"Me, Melinda. I think you ought to know that there's a building moving down Main Street."

"What?" A moment later he was at his door with a lamp in one hand. He had on his long nightshirt.

I said, "Yes, sir. I heard noises and looked out my window, and there's a building moving down Main Street toward the depot."

"What is it? Why would anybody move a building at night? It's long past midnight. I think I'd better see what's going on."

He didn't bother to put on a dressing gown. He started downstairs and out the front door with me at his heels. Out in the street we both stood watching the back end of the building disappear. Then the judge started to run down Cedar Street with me behind him.

When we got to Main, a man on horseback hailed us, yelling, "Hey, Judge, we brought you a present. It's the Heberville courthouse!"

The courthouse! I could only gasp. I recognized the rider as one of the young lawyers who had been at the judge's supper party last week. He and the other men must have gone to Heberville, lifted the small wooden courthouse onto the sledge, and hauled it six miles over the prairie to Goldendale. *They'd stolen the other town's courthouse!*

The judge shouted, "You're crazy drunk, Luke Matthews. Take that back to where it belongs!"

Another young man said, "Ah, we're tired. We thought you'd be tickled to see it, Judge. You want a courthouse, don't you? After all, that's all you've been talking about lately. Well, now you've got one. You're always saying that possession is nine points of the law, aren't you?"

"Thunderation, Phillips, you stole this building! What am I going to do with it?"

Matthews chuckled and said, "It's yours now. We didn't think you'd take our present this way, Judge Garway. We just wanted to cheer you up and tickle your chin whiskers. We'll unhitch the mules and take them back to the livery stable now so you won't have to do it."

Judge Garway bellowed, "You can't just leave that building here!"

Mr. Phillips told him, "We're going to. You can put it wherever you want to. Hide it if you want to. We're going to the all-night saloon for a drink. So long."

The judge and I stood and watched the two men unhitch the mules and lead them away. Then the others rode off after them. Before we knew it, men, mules, and horses were gone. The courthouse stood alone in the center of the street with the judge and me.

I asked, "What're you going to do?"

"Go home, get dressed, and go to that all-night saloon, too. You go back and try to get some sleep, Melinda."

Of course, after that I didn't sleep. I was up and dressed very early, got my own breakfast, and went out to find

Edward Gideon. The judge hadn't come home all night,
and I had a bad feeling that there was going to be a lot
of trouble today over the courthouse. I wanted to have
the judge's dog home with Sarah Jane and me inside the
house. I collared him behind the Pronghorn Hotel. As we
walked home, we passed the Heberville courthouse and
I got a good gander at it. By this time other early risers
were gathering around the building.

As I stood examining it, Esther came running up to me,
followed shortly by Violet from the other end of town.
Stump was already there. He and another boy were climbing up onto its porch, trying to get inside. Suddenly, we
all heard a bugle blowing. *"Toot, wah-h-h, toot!"* It came
again, getting closer.

A moment after the bugle sound, I saw a gray-yellow
dog come hurtling down Main Street. No, not a dog. A
coyote, a big one. He streaked past the courthouse on the
side opposite me and Edward Gideon. The judge's dog
jerked at his leash, but I held tight and yelled at him.

While I struggled, I heard a baying and looked up to
see a whole pack of white-and-brown dogs sweep past
after the coyote. Edward Gideon went wild, pulling and
leaping about. With Violet's help I still hung onto him,
though he knocked us against the courthouse. Then came
a noise like thunder, and a huge bunch of horses with
red-coated riders on them galloped by. They were led by
a man wearing a black top hat, blowing on a bugle. I

knew who they were as soon as I spotted both honourables in the crowd of riders. The men and horses split into two batches and passed the courthouse and us on both sides. This time there just wasn't any holding Edward Gideon. He gave a mighty forward bound, jerked free of Violet and me, and raced down Main Street after the coyote, the dogs, and the horses. I yelled for him to come back, but of course he couldn't possibly have heard me, even with a dog's ears, among all the bugling and screeching of scared townfolk and shouts of the Englishmen.

What was I going to do? Of all times to lose the judge's dog! I had to go after him. I grabbed Esther by the hand, and we hotfooted it to her papa's store. Along the way, I told her what I needed.

As we raced into the store, Esther breathlessly told her father, "Melinda needs Joshua's horse right away! It's already saddled for his errand to Heberville, isn't it?"

"Yes, yes, the horse is still here. So is Joshua. What's going on in town this morning? It's a crazy place. Someone told me there's a building in the middle of Main Street, and a whole crowd of dogs and riders just ran past the store."

While I told the Mittelmans what was going on, Esther ran through to the rear of the store to fetch the horse. Her parents didn't say a word while I spoke. Their eyes just stared into mine like they didn't believe me.

When I saw that Esther had the saddled horse in front,

I shouted "Thank you" to the Mittelmans and ran out. Esther held him steady for me while I got on. Then I kicked him in the sides, held tight with my knees to the saddle and my hands to the reins, and headed out of town for the prairie.

To my disgust, the horse and I were held up for a few minutes at the railroad tracks by the cussed eastbound train just pulling in. Our way was blocked, and we had to wait while passengers got off. This morning there were three ladies and one gent. A gent! I knew him. *Edgar Everett Potter III!* Big as life and carrying two valises. He stared at me from the top of the platform, and I stared back at him from the top of the horse. I wondered if my letter had brought him, but there wasn't time to ask him right now. The train was pulling out, so I gave the horse his head and we skedaddled over the tracks. The hunt was out of sight, but a big cloud of dark-yellow dust ahead showed me where it was going. Two riding lessons weren't enough to make a rider out of me, but all the same I held on to the reins and stayed aboard the horse.

I didn't have any idea how long I chased the hunt before I caught up with it. When I finally reached it, I found it had ended. The riders were milling around, laughing and talking, and Edward Gideon, huge and black, was frolicking about among the hounds. I was pretty embarrassed. My skirt was up over my long, black stockings, and I had no business being with the Englishmen. As I pulled down my skirt, the Honourable Albert saw me and rode over to say, "We lost the coyote, but we had a splendid run all the same!" He acted like I wasn't out of place at all.

I said, "I came to get Judge Garway's dog. You can't miss him. He's the big one in there with the others."

He looked where I pointed and said, "Yes, yes, quite so. The animal is trailing a lead. I'll fetch him to you; or if you prefer, I'll lead him back to town beside my horse."

I looked at Edward Gideon, sighed, and said, "You drag him, please."

By now most of the other red-coated riders were looking at me and smiling. I figured I'd better say something, so I called out, "I only came to get my dog."

While Mr. Albert dismounted and hauled Edward Gideon out of the foxhounds, Mr. Alfred now rode over, greeted me, and began introducing me to some of the guests. He acted just as nice and natural as his brother, and didn't seem at all upset that the sister of the girl who jilted him had busted in on his riding party. I nodded to a duke, two earls, three lords, and some more honourables.

On the ride back, Mr. Alfred asked me, "Wasn't that the Heberville courthouse we rode past on our way through Goldendale?"

"Yes, it arrived last night."

"But how did Goldendale get it?"

"It stole it, sir."

"My word, this truly is still the Wild West! It will be most interesting to learn Heberville's reaction to its loss."

I nodded. He was right about that. The day had just begun, and already I was worn out. I was glad we were riding back to town at a slow pace. Though I'd just galloped over the plains, I wasn't easy with horses; and now, with my horse walking knee-deep in dogs rather than racing along, I started wondering if I'd fall off and break my neck.

We returned to find the courthouse surrounded by people. Some were strangers to me, and I guessed they were Heberville folks. They must have figured where their building had disappeared to and had come to Goldendale to reclaim it. There were enough of them to make a wall of men all around it. Some held rifles. Others had shotguns and pistols.

Judge Garway was there now and so were Mr. Mittelman and two of his sons, Dr. Harmon, Mr. Bauman, Mr. Potter, and a whole bunch of other Goldendale men. Anxious-looking Goldendale ladies stood on the boardwalk. My eyes hunted for Sarah Jane, but I didn't see her, or Edgar Everett III.

What a loud, angry buzzing came from the crowd around the building. As I rode up with the Englishmen, their dogs, and Edward Gideon, I saw a small, fat man being boosted by other men up onto the courthouse porch. He yelled, "I'm Mayor Brown, the mayor of

Heberville. You Goldendale galoots are robbers, pure and simple. You want the county seat and you want our courthouse!"

At these words, everybody started yelling. The English duke next to me said, "How very interesting! So this is the Yankee way of doing things?"

Mr. Alfred told him, "There may be a hurly-burly any moment." As fistfighting broke out in three places in the crowd, he muttered, "Yes, a definite hurly-burly."

I heard the judge's voice booming. *"Stop! Stop this! Nobody shoot!"* Although nobody did shoot, there was pushing and shoving and more fistfights starting up. My horse didn't like it. He began dancing about, threatening to dump me into the crowd of men. He went crashing into Mr. Alfred's bay as a man came pushing through the crowd, waving a piece of yellow paper in one hand. It was the telegraph operator from the depot.

He bellowed, "Judge! Judge Garway, a telegram's just come through from the state capital. They chose the county seat this morning."

Heberville's mayor shouted, "Is it Heberville?"

The telegraph operator shouted back, "No, it's to be Goldendale!"

What a loud hurrah came from the people of Goldendale. It made the horses fidget and fret and the hounds yelp. Among their sharp yelpings I could hear the deep, happy bay of Edward Gideon.

The Heberville men looked sour, and their mayor, who still stood on the courthouse porch, said, "All right, you got the county seat. But this is still our building. You bring it back to us or we get the law on you."

Now I saw Judge Garway and the tall, thin mayor of Goldendale get up onto the courthouse porch, too. Our mayor asked Mayor Brown, "Now that the courthouse is here, what'll you take for it?"

"You mean you want to buy it from us?"

"Why not? I think the good people of Goldendale here would like to subscribe to purchase it."

The Heberville mayor thought for a moment, stooped and spoke with some of his citizens, then straightened up and said, "Two thousand dollars."

The Goldendale mayor told him, "I'll subscribe a hundred of that."

"I'll give a hundred, too," cried Mr. Mittelman.

"Put me down for the same amount," said Dr. Harmon.

After that the offers came in thick and fast until there was fifteen hundred dollars subscribed. Now the Honourable Alfred called out, "My brother and I will give the rest of the money you need."

"God save the queen!" shouted Judge Garway, and everybody laughed, even Heberville folks.

I told Mr. Alfred, "That was nice of you."

"I think it was, too, but the money is well spent. This

whole episode was very interesting. I know it delighted our guests. Your Yankee coyote failed us when it shrewdly ran into a prairie-dog hole, but your way of getting things done was most entertaining for its speed and spirit."

While folks drifted away from the courthouse, I rode over and got Edward Gideon from Mr. Albert. As soon as I delivered the horse to the Mittelmans, I planned to go straight home, not to school at all today. I felt a bit sick.

As I rode off with the dog beside me, I passed Mr. Potter II on the boardwalk. I told him, "Your son's in town. Have you seen him?"

He looked startled and said, "No. Is he?"

"He came in on the morning train." Then I rode on.

I left the horse and walked home fast with Edward Gideon.

I found just what I expected—Edgar Everett Potter III in the judge's parlor with Sarah Jane. They weren't quarreling. They were standing absolutely still, looking at one another. Had they been battling? Were they about to start again?

I held my breath as I stood waiting in the parlor doorway with the dog. Finally I said, "Ah-hum," to break up the silence. I was ready to run out the front door if I had to; I'd left it open just in case.

"Oh, Melinda. Melinda, dear Melinda!" cried Sarah

Jane, and swept up to embrace, not hit, me. She was smiling. She wasn't angry with me. She told me, "It was all a misunderstanding, a terrible one. It's all the fault of his handwriting. He meant *lovely,* not *lonely.* He sends telegrams because his handwriting's so bad. He promises to print from now on. He came to apologize to me because of the dear, sweet, thoughtful letter you wrote him in secret. He showed it to me before he spoke a single word. See, here it is!" And she waved my letter at me.

I looked at her other hand. The amethyst ring was on it again. I stared from it to him. He was grinning widely. I took a deep breath and said, "Mr. Potter, I'm sorry I sent those telegrams. Sarah Jane said to send whatever I felt like sending, and they were how I felt at the time. I feel different now."

He told me, "It's okay. Why don't you send another one, just one, to your folks in Chicago. Tell them your sister and I are getting married here next week. Then we'll go on to California right away."

Sarah Jane added, "And you can go home to Chicago, Melinda."

What a day! An awful lot of things had happened to a lot of people. As Aunt Rhoda always says, "It never rains but it pours!"

Come to think on it, I'd had something to do with so much happening at one time. I hadn't told Judge Garway what I'd overheard his liquored-up guests say after his party. If I had, he probably would have guessed his friends had designs on the Heberville courthouse. I'd been the one who had written to Edgar Everett, so I supposed I shouldn't have been surprised that he would come after Sarah Jane if he really loved her.

The only thing I hadn't had anything to do with was the hunting party. It was the coyote that chose to run through Goldendale. He could have just as easily decided to go through Heberville. I was glad the dogs hadn't caught up to him and that he'd got away.

Dogs! I looked at Edward Gideon, who had just sat down on my left foot.

Sarah Jane was happy now and I was glad for her. The Potters would be pleased about her and their son, and it appeared to me that the Honourable Alfred wasn't grieving over not marrying her. His English friends were enough for him. The judge had his county seat and his courthouse, although there was still the matter of Edward Gideon's roaming.

And then there was me, Melinda! I hadn't planned to return home to Chicago so suddenly. Going away so unexpectedly upset me. I didn't want to leave my Colorado friends. I'd miss the Mittelman family, and in Chicago I'd be thinking about Mrs. Mittelman's loneliness. It would be very sad for her if Esther left home to go away to school and study to be a rabbi.

I sighed as I went into the kitchen with Edward

Gideon and got a beef bone for him from the icebox. I left him busy with it in the backyard and walked away to the telegraph office.

The Heberville courthouse hadn't been moved. School kids were climbing all over it. Stump came by and circled me on his bicycle as I stopped again to look at the courthouse on Main Street.

"There ain't any school today. Miss Hawkins said there was too much excitement here to try to teach anything."

"Thank you, Walter," I said and went on to the depot, leaving him staring after me because I'd been so pleasant and used his real name.

There I sent Aunt Rhoda and Uncle Julius my last telegram from Goldendale: "Edgar forgiven. Marrying here. Them to California—me to Chicago." I'd write them the details later tonight. Right now all I wanted to do was get back to Cedar Street and lie down in my room. This had been a very wearying morning.

II

Some Surprises!

Esther and Violet were truly downcast after I told them that I was leaving. They were glad everything had come out all right in the end for Sarah Jane and Edgar Everett, and they admired my nerve in sending him a letter. But they sure didn't want me to leave, even though they knew that I couldn't stay here by myself. Besides, Aunt Rhoda kept writing about how empty her house was without me clumping down the stairs and making my usual noises.

Esther mourned. "Mama and I will miss you, Melinda. Mama says you and Edward Gideon make her laugh. She liked talking with you whenever you came into the store or dropped by our house."

I nodded and said, "I like your folks, Esther. I hope someday you get a *minyan* here."

"Maybe we will, but Papa says that some towns never

get one. Melinda, we'll write to one another, won't we?"

"Oh, sure we will. I'm giving up telegrams. You can't say enough in them. Say, do you know anybody who could take over dog-sitting Edward Gideon for the judge? I think it ought to be somebody younger than me." As I said this, I looked hard at Violet, who was a half year younger than I was.

For a long time my two friends pondered, then Violet said, "Nope. It takes a responsible kid as well as a strong one with sturdy arms. That dog was an awful trial when I fetched him home to the judge. You did it better than I did."

That let Violet out.

Esther said next, "I couldn't do it. Remember, I don't go out much on Saturdays."

We all sighed under our cottonwood tree.

I wondered if Stump Wood would miss me when I left, and if he'd ever tell me that he was madly in love with me. I doubted he would. I suspected now that he had loved me at first sight. I could remember that first day he set eyes on me as I sat on the porch of the Pronghorn Hotel waiting for Sarah Jane. How he had stared! It hadn't been only that I was a new kid in town. There had to be something to love at first sight, though it sure had its dangers, too. As Judge Garway said, don't be hasty.

Although Edgar Everett was staying with his parents

until the wedding, he might as well have been living at the judge's house, he called there so often on the telephone. The conversations were mostly mush or about the wedding arrangements. When I answered the three long rings and one short that meant the party-line call was for the judge, sometimes I shouted for Sarah Jane before I even heard his hello. It was always Edgar.

Just as I came into the hallway with Edward Gideon after watching the Englishmen's railroad cars pull out of town on Tuesday afternoon, the phone rang. I answered it, and as I figured, it was Edgar Everett. I told the judge's dog to sit while I went to find my sister. She was in the kitchen rolling out pie crust, with flour all over her hands and arms.

When I told her it was Edgar Everett again, she said, "Please tell him to call me later. I can't come to the phone just now."

"Okay, I will," I said, and went back into the hallway. Edward Gideon was still sitting down beside the wall phone with the receiver on its long cord swinging back and forth next to him. His head was cocked toward it. I'd heard him bark once while I was in the kitchen. Now he barked again.

I picked up the receiver and asked, "Hey, were you talking to the judge's dog just now, Mr. Potter? I heard him barking."

He laughed and said, "Sure. I heard him bark. Then I

heard him snuffling, so I asked him how he was doing these days, and he barked again. Then you came onto the line."

"Mr. Potter, did *you* ask him to *bark* for you?" I asked excitedly.

"Yep, and he did it, too! He's a smart dog."

"Mr. Potter, would you ask Edward Gideon to sit down now? Please say it loud."

"Okay, I'll yell."

I held the receiver out to Edward Gideon. *"Sit down, dog!"* came thundering through the phone.

Edward Gideon sat down!

I sucked in my breath and mentally thanked Alexander Graham Bell. After also thanking Edgar Everett and telling him to call Sarah Jane back later, I hung up, grabbed Edward Gideon's leash, and ran out of the house with him. We ran all the way to Mittelman's Emporium, where I spoke with Mrs. Mittelman and Esther. At first they looked startled when I explained what I wanted, then they laughed and promised to keep hold of Edward Gideon for me beside the telephone.

I ran back to Cedar Street. To my joy I found Judge Garway had just come in. I told him what I had in mind and saw how his Lincolnlike sad eyes lit up with interest. Then he said, "Well, I suppose it's worth a try, isn't it?"

I stood in the hallway as he asked the lady operator to

put him through to Mittelman's Emporium. When she connected him, he said, "This is Judge Garway. Esther, is it? Well, I understand my dog is there with you. He is? Good. Will you please put him on the line. Thank you."

In the pause that followed, Sarah Jane came out of the kitchen. Before she could ask me why I was listening to the judge's telephone conversation, I put my finger to my lips and said, "Sh-h, he's going to talk to Edward Gideon in just a minute."

"*What?*"

And then the judge took over. "*Edward Gideon,*" he thundered. "*Dog!* You know my voice! I am your master! You come home at once. Don't you stop anywhere along the way—not at a saloon or the barbershop or pool hall. Come straight home, sir! Come home, *Edward Gideon!*"

The judge hung up, turned to face the two of us, and said, "Now we wait. I am hoping against hope that my telephone voice will affect him because it is different from the voice he normally hears. Telephone voices are more metallic. He may pay more attention to me over the line than he does in person. Seeing me could distract him, you know." He sighed and looked at the ceiling.

We waited together in the parlor, the judge looking at his pocket watch and finger-drumming on the table next to him, Sarah Jane crocheting on a potholder, and me biting at a hangnail. It seemed that we waited for a whole hour before we heard a barking, then the sound of toenails scratching at the front door. Dog toenails! Edward Gideon had done it. He'd come home, and by the front door, too. The judge didn't need a private dog-catcher anymore. All he needed was a list of telephone numbers and a bit of patience.

Sarah Jane's wedding was set for Sunday afternoon. I was to be my sister's bridesmaid, so I'd get to wear the pale green dress I'd brought from Chicago after all. I decided I didn't want a calla lily in my sash like Aunt Rhoda had suggested. I thought my dress would look nicer if I could wear a water lily instead. I'd read that this was the latest spring fashion in New York.

My mind was on water lilies and where to find one as I went to the drugstore with Esther and Violet on Wednesday. They were treating me to a farewell ice-cream soda because I'd be leaving on the eastbound train on Monday morning. Just as we reached Bauman's door, Dr. Harmon came out and collared us, saying, "Just a minute, girls. I've just been showing Jake a letter I got today. I think you'll be interested in it, too, particularly you, Esther."

I asked, "Who's it from?"

"It's from a doctor in New York City. I went to

medical school with him forty years ago. He treats tuberculosis and other diseases of the lungs." He was grinning
at us.

I couldn't see why this should make anybody smile, but
I kept quiet.

He went on. "I wrote my friend about the pure air and
good water here, and—"

Violet interrupted, "Why did you do that? The water
here tastes awful!" She was right. I wouldn't miss the
water one bit.

He said, "That is true, but it's good for your gizzards.
Well, my friend is thinking of opening a small sanatorium
somewhere in the West. He'd send his patients to it to get
them out of the city. The hospital he has in mind would
have a population of about twenty or thirty men and
women. It would be a special sort of sanatorium."

"What kind?" asked Esther quickly.

"One for Jewish people. The doctor is Jewish. On the
strength of the letter I wrote him, he's coming out here
next month to look Goldendale over as a site for his
sanatorium."

I saw Esther clap her hands to the sides of her face. She
cried, "Oh, it could be our *minyan*! If there're to be
twenty or thirty people, there will surely be five men,
wouldn't there?"

"Probably," agreed the doctor, "but it'd be a floating

population, with people coming and going all the time."

"That'd be all right," said Esther. "That doesn't matter. What matters is ten men. Have you told my parents about this yet?"

"Not yet, just Jake Bauman. I thought I'd tell your folks later this afternoon. Or would you rather tell them now, Esther?"

Esther didn't say a word. She whirled around and started pell-mell for the Emporium, with Violet running after her. I would have gone, too, but Dr. Harmon called to me. "Melinda, as an afterthought, I think I'll go over to the *Goldendale Press* now and tell my friend, the editor, that the New York City doctor's coming out to see if he wants to invest some capital in the town. He'll find that news fit to print, I'm sure."

I said, "Probably so. I hear they're going to put a piece in next Monday's paper about my sister marrying Edgar Everett Potter III. Esther's promised to cut out the notice and mail it to me in Chicago."

Dr. Harmon said, "Yes, I guess when your sister goes away with young Potter, you leave, too. Goldendale will miss you, Melinda. You've livened it up for a time with all your antics. I've watched you in snow and hail and sleet, in sunshine and rain, with that big dog of the judge's in tow or with him towing you. I have quite enjoyed knowing you, Miss Carpenter, and I am sure the judge has, too." He tipped his hat to me and crossed the street, leaving me basking in compliments.

When I got to Mittelman's, I found everybody thrilled at the doctor's news. Of course, the judge and Sarah Jane were just as happy when I told them about the sanatorium later. Sarah Jane said it would be a fine thing for city folks to breath good Colorado air, and the judge added that it would put the state's "healthful climate even more on the map."

We went to dinner at the Potter home that night. Mr. and Mrs. Potter didn't seem too interested in the sanatorium. I could understand why—their minds were on the wedding and my sister, not on me or what I might say. Oh, they were pleasant enough to me, but I had a feeling they weren't going to miss me when I was gone. I think I'm a little too lively for two old folks like them to really understand. I couldn't forget what Mr. Potter had said to the honourable about me that one time—that I was not a mere child. That was true, of course. I wasn't. I had never been. And I was proud of it.

Thursday's edition of the *Goldendale Press* ran Dr. Harmon's story about the visiting Jewish doctor and his sanatorium plans. We all read the article and discussed it after dinner. Then Sarah Jane went with Edgar Everett to a vaudeville performance. I stayed home reading *Ivanhoe* and was there in the parlor when the judge telephoned the

Bonanza Palace Saloon for Edward Gideon at nine o'-
clock. We waited together until he came home twenty
minutes later, then I took him outside to the backyard and
watched him leap the fence at once. It appeared to me that
Edward Gideon was enjoying his telephone calls as much
as the judge.

I didn't look forward to my last day of school on
Friday, because I expected it to be a dull and sad time for
me. After all, I wouldn't see Miss Hawkins or Stump or
any of the other kids again except for Esther and Violet,
who were coming to the wedding. Just before lunch, Miss
Hawkins made a little speech about having enjoyed me
in her school and wishing me well. Then she insisted that
all the kids sing "Auld Lang Syne" to me, which made
me blush with pleasure.

During recess I waited under the cottonwood for
Stump to come talk to me privately, but he didn't. He
stayed with the other boys, stubbing the toe of his boot
over and over into the dust. He even kept his back to me.

Suddenly, Esther, Violet, and I saw Gar and his brother
coming toward us. Gar looked like an angry bull let loose
in a pasture. He lumbered up, looking very mean, and
told Esther, "I wish it was you leavin' town, Essie Mittelman, with yer pal from Chicago."

Violet flared at him, "What do you mean?"

Gar shouted now so everybody could hear him. "I told you before. Me and my folks don't want no more Jewish people to come to Goldendale. Pa read in the newspaper yesterday that maybe more Jewish people'll be coming here. We already got enough with you Mittelmans and old Bauman, the druggist. Pa says that's too many already." Now Gar pushed me into Esther.

Violet put her arms around Esther, who had turned pale and looked like she might scream or run or start to cry. Violet knew what to do.

So did I! I let out a yell and slapped Gar across the cheek. In return he slammed me against the cottonwood so hard it knocked the breath out of me and made tears flood my eyes.

When I was able to see again, I could make out Stump. He had Gar by the suspenders and was jerking him around. One of Stump's friends had Gar's brother fast by the arm. Though Gar was bigger than he was, Stump seemed stronger. He tossed the bully out, pulled him in by his suspenders and punched him, then tossed him out again. Gar punched, too. Once when he broke free, he reached down and threw some dirt into Stump's face, but he didn't do too much damage. Stump was a good dodger, even with dirt in his eyes. Finally Stump knocked Gar to the ground, stepped over him, and sat down hard on his stomach.

Holding his fist inches from Gar's nose, Stump said, "This is a free country. Folks in America come where they want to come and go where they want to go. Nobody says that they can't move around as they please. Now, Gar, you just lay there and think about what I just said."

I looked at Esther, who had her head buried in Violet's shoulder. Then I looked back at Stump. I took my handkerchief out of my pocket, went over to him, and wiped the dirt off his face. With all of the kids looking on, he lifted his face to me and let me wipe it. He didn't even shove me away when I whispered softly into his ear, "Walter Wood, you are a great big hero, the biggest I ever set eyes on. Thank you for your valentine. I saw you leave it on my front porch." He was grinning at me as I went on. "If I write you a letter from Chicago, I'd like it fine if you'd answer it."

Just as Miss Hawkins ran over and started to yell, "*Walter*, get off that boy and let him get up!" Stump nodded.

That's all he did, nod, but I knew! I knew he'd answer me and then I'd write him again. Just like I'd write Esther and Violet. As I stepped back from him, I stuffed my handkerchief into the top pocket of his overalls. I'd given him a token of my favor the way ladies did in *Ivanhoe*. It was one of my best handkerchiefs, the one with blue forget-me-nots embroidered in the corners. By accident it had the right flowers on it.

I watched him get up off Gar and shove my handkerchief farther down so no one would spot it. Then he walked away like he hadn't done anything heroic at all.

As the three of us girls started for the schoolhouse followed by a hangdog Gar and his brother, Esther said in a soft voice, "Thank you, Melinda. Gar gave you a bad time, too, didn't he?"

I put one arm on her shoulder and the other arm about Violet's waist and said, "Yes, it was bad, and I won't forget it. But I'm pretty sure Gar won't open his mouth to say anything like that again. If he does, Stump will see to him. Esther, most folks here like you and your family just fine. You're a very important part of Goldendale." I went on. "I'm glad I got stuck here with Sarah Jane because I got to meet the two of you. I'd rather know you any day than honourables or dukes or earls. I'll remember the two of you and hope to see you someday again." I sighed. "You know, I think I'll quit taking a hand in other people's business when I get back home. But I have to tell you that I'm glad I took one in a few things around here now and then—like the *minyan* sign that got Dr. Harmon going, and the swoon that got me to see a real castle, and the letter I wrote that brought Mr. Potter here to make my sister happy."

"Those were nice things," said Violet.

"Yes, I'm glad you took a hand now and then," came from Esther. "When you're gone, Violet and I may start to take a hand in things hereabouts, too. We'll try to get Judge Garway a nice, new housekeeper."

I told them, "Just remember one thing if you do. Don't be hasty! That's a verdict from the judge."

Esther laughed and so did Violet, but I laughed most of all.

Sarah Jane and Edgar Everett Potter III got hitched that Sunday without a single hitch. Judge Garway, looking every tall inch like Abe Lincoln, offered to give my sister away and went down the aisle with her on his arm at four o'clock like he was our real father. I couldn't see Sarah Jane's face because of the wedding veil, but I knew she was smiling.

We'd talked Friday night about love at first sight, and she'd told me that sometimes it happened. She said that it could take even sensible people, meaning me, by rude surprise. She hoped when it came to me, it would grow slowly and politely and would last. Well, I hoped for that, too.

I was her maid of honor and I wore my pale green muslin dress. There weren't any water-lily ponds near Goldendale, so Esther made me a white-and-green-silk one to wear in my sash. I looked lovely, although I must say that the dress was now a bit too short and tight, because I'd put on some inches in Goldendale in two directions. I was growing up. After all, I'd very soon be fourteen. By the end of summer, I'd have my hair up on top of my head and my skirts down to my ankles like a grown-up.

Edgar Everett Potter looked nice in a dark suit and high collar that brushed the tips of his ears, but I thought he almost started choking when he said, "I do."

Although I tried to keep my eyes fixed on the preacher, the bride and groom, the judge, and Edgar Everett's best man, Mr. Potter II, I couldn't help glancing over my shoulder at the people behind us. Mrs. Potter II sat in a front pew, dolled up in purple lace and a big, violet-colored hat with white-ostrich-plume wings on each side. She was crying and wiped her eyes with a handkerchief over and over. I wondered if those were tears of relief at her boy's finally getting married or because she always cried at weddings the way Aunt Rhoda did.

Violet Stowe and all of her family, dressed in their Sunday best, sat in the pew behind Mrs. Potter, nodding and smiling. There were also some church folks Sarah Jane and I knew and some Potter friends we didn't know.

Esther and her family weren't there, but she'd called me that morning on the telephone to tell me that her water lily would represent her at the ceremony. It was sticking into my stomach, so I was reminded of her the entire time.

She was there outside the church when we all came out, and her mother was with her. Beside Esther sat Edward Gideon with a huge white moire bow around his neck.

It set off his sleek, black coat just fine. Esther had brushed him and washed him and put the bow on him to please me. Well, I was pleased! Mrs. Mittelman came up to me, smiling, and I noticed that she had a small basket over her arm. She gave Violet and me little red-and-white-striped bags from the basket with the words, "It's for the bride and groom."

I looked inside. Rice! I'd been at weddings before, so I knew what rice was for. I ran down the church steps with Violet and Esther, and when Sarah Jane and Edgar Everett came out together, we all pelted them with the rice. Then Mr. and Mrs. Potter III got into a buggy to go to the Pronghorn Hotel, where the wedding supper was to be. They'd stay at the hotel until their train left at seven-thirty in the morning. I was staying at the hotel, too, and would leave on the eight o'clock train in the other direction.

"Mazel tov!" cried both Mittelmans after the newly-weds.

Esther shouted to me, "That means congratulations!"

Judge Garway had stayed at the top of the church steps. Now he came down to stand next to me as my sister and her husband drove off. I looked up at him and pointed to Edward Gideon, who was lumbering over to sit down beside us now that the rice throwing was over. He'd done a good bit of barking while that was going on. I told the judge, "He came, too! Doesn't he look grand, though?"

"Very grand," agreed the judge. Then he added, "Well, it seems that I've not only given away a bride, but given away a housekeeper, too. What'll I do now?"

"Get another housekeeper."

"In time, I'm sure I shall. Well, Melinda, I'm happy that your sister is over her sorrow. She moped considerably lately—until you wrote a letter to young Potter." As I looked up at him in surprise, he went on. "Yes, she told me all about your letter." He cleared his throat. "*Your* writing the letter was not entirely what I had in mind when I said I would ask Potter for clarification. You took it on yourself. Oh, well, all's well that ends well, as the poet says."

"As Shakespeare says."

"That's right, Shakespeare. So, you'll leave for Chicago tomorrow, eh, and I'll be going to the Pronghorn Hotel for my meals again and summoning my dog by telephone. I will miss your company and that of your sister as much as I will miss her cooking."

I said, "We'll miss you, too. I hope she told you that. You know, Judge, from now on when I read the Chicago papers, I'll keep my eyes peeled for any news about Colorado. That way I'll know when you become governor, and after that a United States senator."

"Do that, Melinda, do that. I'd be happy if you would,

but please allow me twenty years to accomplish everything."

"Oh, you'll do it in fifteen, I bet. Unless I miss my
guess, you'll have a new housekeeper, too, pretty soon."

"And how is that to happen?"

I gestured toward Esther and Violet, who were return-
ing the empty rice sacks to Mrs. Mittelman. I said, "My
friends promised me yesterday that they were going to
take a hand in that for you."

"Those two girls? How will they do that?"

I told him, "The Chicago way. My way. It's a surprise.
Be prepared."

No, I didn't want to spoil the surprise by telling him
that just as soon as I left town, Esther and Violet planned
to make a sign and put it up on the depot wall. It was
to say:

GENEROUS-PAYING BACHELOR JUDGE NEEDS LADY
HOUSEKEEPER. ASK FOR JUDGE JEDEDIAH GARWAY, 48
CEDAR STREET.

The three of us had pooled our chores money to pay
in advance for the spot on the depot wall, so the stationmaster wouldn't come asking Judge Garway to pay like
he'd done to Mr. Mittelman. It was all figured out, and
we hadn't been one bit hasty about it either.

Now Judge Garway, Edward Gideon, and I walked up to my friends, the Potter parents, the rest of the wedding guests, and the preacher and his wife. When we were all together, I told them all, "Let's go down to the Pronghorn where the wedding supper's due to start real soon!"

❦Author's Note❧

Goldendale is fictional, a composite of some 1890's Colorado towns I have researched in several libraries. Prairie *cum* mountain locales could be a feature of a number of the actual communities.

Historically, 1893 was a year of depression. In 1894, the year in which this story ends, an army of the unemployed, called Coxey's Army after the man who organized it, marched on Washington, D.C. Wages and prices in 1893 were very different from today's. A man's good shirt could sell for twenty cents. A month's very good wages could be fifty dollars. A full-length sealskin coat could cost fifteen dollars. Working in 1893 was different, too. Hours were much longer and the work harder because there were fewer machines. I set a figure of two thousand dollars for a courthouse. Today it sounds ridiculous, but not in 1893, when it represented a great deal of money.

1893 was the year of the Great Exposition in Chicago. Millions of people attended from all over the world. One of the real exhibits from the state of California was a sculpture of a knight and rider made from prunes. I do not know if it was gilded or not, but I make it so. The old newspapers I read of the era did not specify. In them I found some very modern-sounding words, like *pal* and *okay*.

To many readers it will no doubt seem extremely unlikely that there would be upper-class Englishmen living in the Far West—not to mention riding to hounds in red coats in pursuit of a coyote. There is no contrivance on my part here. Many English people, remittance men among them, came to the American West in the 1880's and 1890's, bringing culture and capital with them. Those inclined to hunting hunted mightily—deer, bear, buffalo, and coyotes. Wagons transported hounds onto the prairie in cages, and the dogs were set loose when a coyote was sighted. The wealthy English gave lengthy house parties for guests from Britain and endeavored to maintain British customs, such as afternoon tea, croquet, polo, and tennis. Some of the young gentlemen were quite disorderly. (In Riverside, California, they once rode polo ponies into a dining room, circling the table of diners.)

Speaking of the British, transplanted castles such as the one described here were found in parts of the United

States, though not all were reconstructed on the prairie. Stones from castles in England, Scotland, and Ireland were marked, crated, shipped to America, and set up— just as London Bridge was set up at Lake Havasu in Arizona fairly recently. Not all castles were owned by the English, however. Some were purchased by rich Americans hankering for ancestral halls and inspired by the very popular novels of Sir Walter Scott. No one, so far as I have ever heard, has made the claim that medieval castles were comfortable dwellings. They were damp, drafty, and generally cold.

The episode of the purloined courthouse may also seem to be a wild figment of my imagination. Not so! During the last century a group of energetic, enterprising pranksters in the Pacific Northwest put the courthouse of a neighboring county onto a sledge and hauled it over the county line to get the county seat designation. I do not know if they paid the owners, but I presume they did. These thieves went my Goldendale thieves one better. The historical building was conveyed over a river! To add to this, the story of the traveling house made to hoodwink inspectors of homesteads is factual.

I have also referred to prefabricated houses. They were very commonly erected in some parts of the West. They were bought by model number from a catalog and arrived as precut lumber. Railway stations, schoolhouses, stores, and churches, as well as private residences, could be mail-ordered.

In this novel, I have given my heroine the job of private dogcatcher. I took the idea from a piece I once read about a man who was deeply distressed over the wandering behavior of his dog, which he considered to be a town tramp. Somehow he learned that the dog would come home on his own when loudly ordered to do so over the telephone. So the man summoned him home from wherever he found him by calling. He would ask that the dog be put on the line, then shout for him to head for home and not stop along the way.

My heroine's swoon was quite in order as something ladies did in 1893. Tightly laced corsets could lead to them, as did emotional shocks. However, more than a few swoons were staged efforts to get attention. The literature of the day is full of such behavior. Well-bred ladies in novels were constantly at it and constantly being revived by well-bred gentlemen on both sides of the Atlantic Ocean. Though Colorado women had the vote in 1893, years before the constitutional amendment was adopted, they still swooned.

My fictional Sarah Jane becomes distraught and sad when she confuses the written word *lovely* with *lonely*. This exact confusion took place between a real nine-teenth-century young woman and the man who wrote to her. The true story doesn't have a happy ending, however. She married someone else. It was not until some years had passed that she found out she'd misread the handwriting.

I have written here something of the lives of Jewish people who settled in the West. Many of them were former wagon peddlers who married and found themselves the only Jewish family in a town when they opened stores or professional offices. Jews did not experience the prejudice in the West that they sometimes found in the East and in Europe, but they suffered from isolation and they found it difficult to keep to Jewish ways. Keeping Saturday, a busy commercial day, a holy day would be near to impossible. So would ritual worship. A *minyan* of ten men over the age of thirteen is required by Jewish law before Jews can worship publicly, build a temple, or buy a burial ground. Many frontier towns never secured enough men for a *minyan*.

I have described a *Shabbes,* or Sabbath, supper with the aid of Jewish friends. I've also spoken of Esther Mittelman's dream of becoming a woman rabbi. This did not happen in fact until 1972, but in 1893 a remarkable, highly educated Jewish woman named Rachel Frank was actually preaching in synagogues in California. She was a journalist, editor, and theologian who was offered the post of rabbi in Chicago in 1893 but refused it, saying that the place of the Jewish woman was in the home. Born in

1866, she died in 1948. She is best known by her married name, Ray Frank Litman. (My Esther could have become another Rachel Frank.)

I have mentioned the possibility of a sanatorium in my fictional Goldendale. Spas were sprouting up all over the West in the 1870's through the 1890's. Colorado's medicinal waters and pure air drew asthmatics and tuberculosis patients to the state. A Jewish organization, the Jewish Consumptive Relief Society, opened a sanatorium in Denver in the 1870's.

Young readers may wonder at Melinda's sending telegrams when there was a telephone system in Goldendale and in Chicago. Long-distance calls could be made between cities such as Boston and New York as early as 1884, but it was not until 1911 that Denver was connected with Eastern cities by long distance. Issues of 1893 newspapers gave me these facts. They also gave me some others that may seem farfetched, but are true. In a June, 1893, edition of *The New York Times* there appeared not only the story of the tightrope walker crossing Niagara Falls with the cookstove, but the one of the escaped lion and helpful elephant, and the amazingly recompensed Texas milk-cow race.

In writing this novel for young people, I have had a good bit of help from a number of people. I wish to thank the librarians at both the University of California, River-

side library, and the Riverside Public Library—in particular, librarians Ruth Halman and Laine Farley. I would
also like to thank friends who helped me with the details
of the *Shabbes* supper—Devera Stewart, Dorothy Leon,
Sara Reznick, and Leah Nessen.

                              Patricia Beatty
                              July, 1982

About the Author

Now a resident of Southern California, Patricia Beatty was born in Portland, Oregon. She was graduated from Reed College there, and then taught high-school English and history for four years. Later she held various positions as science and technical librarian and also as a children's librarian. Quite recently she has taught Writing Fiction for Children in the Extension Department of the University of California, Los Angeles. She has had a number of historical novels published by Morrow, several of them dealing with the American West in the 1860 to 1895 period.

With her late husband, Dr. John Beatty, Mrs. Beatty also coauthored a number of books. One of them, *The Royal Dirk,* was chosen as an Award Book by the Southern California Council on Children's and Young People's Literature. Subsequently, Mrs. Beatty received another award from the Council for her Distinguished Body of Work.

Mrs. Beatty is now married to a professor of economics at the University of California, Riverside, and has a married daughter, Alexandra Beatty Stewart.